when luke met juliette

THE ENERGY SERIES
BOOK 1

BROOKELYN MOSLEY

85 MEDIA LLC

contents

message from the author

Thank you for purchasing your copy of *When Luke Met Juliette*. This story is a standalone divided into two-parts with a conclusion once you reach the end.

Though this story represents book one in a series (The Energy Series), *When Luke Met Juliette* is a complete standalone, meaning book two in the Energy Series will not be about them. To my knowledge, there are no trigger warnings to report. However, I need to note that *When Luke Met Juliette* contains sexually explicit content and profanity in dialogue. If you are sensitive to the previously mentioned, this book may not fit the reading experience you are looking for.

If all is well and you are ready to dive in, thank you again for choosing *When Luke Met Juliette* for your reading entertainment.

Enjoy the rivalry!

Love,
BK

acknowledgments

A loving thank you to my amazing husband who is without a doubt one of my biggest supporters. Your support is worth its weight in gold. A special thank you to my reading family and early supporters of my work. I'm sure you've noticed the changes; you've even commented on it. I thank you for sticking beside me and growing with me. You all have embraced my brand of writing and I'm beyond appreciative of it. Shout out to the readers who have reached out to me to share your thoughts regarding my books. I thank you for keeping me motivated and excited to create new projects for you. When I write, I keep you in mind. Thank you for your support. It's my soul food.

JULIETTE

"THIS WILL BE the last time I ever run an errand like this again. I swear. *Ugh!*"

I leaned over my rear bumper to stretch my arm into the back of my trunk to gather the last of the red party cups. The red cups were a part of the abnormally large party supply errand my cheer squad delegated to me to handle at the last minute for our pre-game party that night.

"Not that I had a choice." I sighed, relieved at the momentary victory of securing the last of the red cups in my grip. "Freshman obligations, my ass."

I was supposed to handle the errand with two other girls, also freshman, but last-minute studying for make-up exams had them choose books over booze to pass their classes during their very first semesters at Brookville.

It was dark out that night. The hour after 9pm. Out here in Long Island, New York, when the hour dipped below 5pm, so did the temperature. It was cold outside. My exhales through my nose were leaving behind long plumes of white smoke in the air.

The brisk breeze nipped at my bare fingertips as I swiped my hand inside my trunk, double checking I'd gotten all the cups out of the car.

There were still Styrofoam plates and plastic shot glasses remaining, but I wasn't hauling all that into our school's student lounge, where the party would take place. The rest of my cheer squad would have to trek back to my car with me to get what remained. I was done, and I wasn't about to be the party mule. I already had to wait in line at checkout for close to half an hour at the only party store in town. I'd done enough.

And I wasn't trippin'. Because in less than an hour, I could drown my annoyance in a cup of our head cheerleader, Toni's, spiked Ville Juice, a signature at Brookville U, that I learned was more rum than juice. Which enticed an 18-year-old Juliette.

I fought back a smile, lifting my arms to grab the top of the trunk's door to close with plans to head toward the doors of the building housing our student lounge.

Out of sync, rhythmic thuds like the sound feet made from pounding pavement echoed against the asphalt ground behind me, but it was too cold and I was too through with the task at hand to care.

So I ignored it, even as the thuds increased in pace and volume, growing nearer.

In this quiet ass town, there was nothing to be worried about, anyway. People in the small town of Brookville, New York slept in houses with unlocked doors. That's how safe Brookville was. So best believe the thuds didn't alarm me. If anything, I figured they had to be on the basketball team or cheer squad, since we were the only ones out on this side of campus at that hour. So, they could help me lug the rest of the supplies into the school.

Just as I turned to glance over my shoulder and in the noise's direction, my right shoulder went careening forward as someone bumped me from behind. The bulk of the red cups flew out of my hands next and fell all around me as three towering bodies went racing by me on foot.

The thuds I heard belonged to three pairs of rubber bottom sneakers. The three guys wearing them stampeded by me, also wearing royal blue hoodies and matching joggers.

My jaw dropped and eyes widened. I ripped my eyes off them to find half of the drinking cups on the parking lot's asphalt ground.

I was seconds away from yelling a couple of *"what the fuck?"* and a few *"you stupid pieces of shit"* at them when one of the three, the one who bumped into me, stopped running feet away.

"Shit," he hissed, jogging back to me.

"Nah, LL," one of them shouted. "Let's go. We gotta go right now!"

There was a black Suburban truck waiting up ahead with bright red taillights and a steaming exhaust.

"Luke, bring yo' ass!" the other instructed. "Forget her."

But Luke didn't listen.

He moved around me, snatching up the bulk packages of red cups super quick.

"Luke, come on!" another shouted.

"Man, give me a fucking minute, damn," Luke shouted back at them.

I parked beneath one of the parking lot lights, so when Luke removed the blue hood from off his head, I got a dim but perfect view of his face as he neared.

Sincere eyes encased in milky dark brown skin and lips framed by a perfectly trimmed black mustache and goatee combo. The clearest complexion I'd ever seen in a guy my age. He was tall, with broad shoulders and long, lean arms. While I struggled to hold the bulk pack of cups, his arms cradled the cups like it was nothing.

The scent of fresh laundry invaded my space when he approached. An invasion that was more than welcomed.

We locked eyes, and he smirked.

He handed the bulk pack of cups to me when he was close and said, "My bad, shorty. It's dark out here and your car is off. Didn't see you. You good?"

I pressed the plastic packaging to my chest, eyes unwavering, because my God in heaven.

Luke had the accent I heard in those Golden Age hip hop songs I blasted in my dorm room. Hip hop songs I've been blasting since my freshman year in high school. That Kool G Rap, Nas, KRS-One, Big Daddy Kane.

He had a signature deep city boy inflection in his deep raspy voice. An inflection nurtured beneath the skyscraper lights in one of those New York City boroughs and grown through the cracks between the gritty concrete. All of which I've wanted so badly to be around since my parents opened their first business in Brooklyn. In the few words he spoke to me, he said them in the deepest, richest, raspiest voice I'd ever heard.

He was my version of Prince Charming.

"*Mm-hmm,*" I replied with a nod, because that was the only way I could respond. I couldn't activate my vocal cords long enough to say anything else in that instance. My heart was no better. The muscle was trying to fight its way out of my chest and escape into his arms so it could run away with him into the moonlight.

I don't know *what* it was doing, honestly.

What I know is that in that moment, out in that dim parking lot, with his band of misfits hollering for him to get in the truck from feet away, Luke was the guy I'd fantasized about meeting when I imagined going to college. Not necessarily at Brookville, but shit, good enough.

"Yeah, you're good." He smiled at my inability to speak and

licked his lips slow. His eyes twinkled when he added, "You look good, too."

I took a breath and released it with a sigh.

His eyes shifted off me, and his smile contorted into a shocked O.

"You asshole!" I heard Toni scream from behind me.

I turned in time to see Toni throw her white Nike sneaker in our direction, that I dodged out of the way of.

My attention returned to Luke, who laughed as he jogged away backwards, creating a distance between us.

"I fucking hate y'all so much!" Toni hollered.

It was dark, but I could make out the pissed expression on Toni's face.

"Oh, you *love* us, shorty, and you know it," Luke shouted back, turning to run toward the Suburban.

Toni was on his tail, running not too far behind. "Eat a dick."

"You first, baby," Luke countered.

Toni grunted, stopping short to snatch off her other Nike sneaker to throw like a dart at the Suburban. The sneaker spun in the air and collided with one of the lit taillights, causing no damage.

Luke and the other guys in the car heckled her reaction with boisterous laughter.

Right before climbing into the truck, he told me, "See you tomorrow, shorty," winking then ducking into the backseat. Less than a second later, the truck went speeding out of the university parking lot, leaving behind tire markings and the echoes of screeching wheels as the Suburban's taillights appeared to fade into the dark night.

Toni swiped up her Nikes off the ground one by one, mumbling expletives to herself as she made her way to me.

"Girl." I glanced over her shoulder, and in the direction Luke and his crew drove off in. I was hoping to get another glimpse of the vehicle carrying my new crush in the backseat. "Who the hell was *that?*"

"*Hell*, is the perfect word because *that* demon," she spat, out of breath, "is Luke freakin' Lockett."

I bit my bottom lip. "I think I'm feelin' him."

"No." She stopped in front of me. "You *know* you *hate* him. You hate him a lot."

I hoisted the bulk pack of cups in my arms and balanced them on one side of my waist. "Huh?"

"See?" She pointed at me. "See?! I know for a fact now you don't pay attention during practice. I get you've only been a student here for just four months, but come on! We've mentioned him more than enough times, Juliette."

Of course I don't pay attention, Toni. Cheer squad practice is the perfect place to space out because we barely practice, duh.

"I pay attention," I insisted anyway.

"Oh, yeah?" She challenged, folding her arms. "Then how come as soon as I identified him as Luke Lockett, your mind didn't think of Langston University?"

"Langston U? Why would it…?" I tilted my head to one side. "Wait. He goes to Langston?"

"*Yes*, you fool. That's Luke Lockett from Langston U and him and his crew of ghetto assholes just ruined our damn night."

"How?"

She groaned, dropping her head back between her shoulders, messing up the order of her perfectly arranged locs. "He and the two other players he came with somehow got into the arena with two members from their cheer squad and spray-painted *LU WINS!* in big blue letters on both backboards on *our* basketball court."

My jaw dropped. "What? Why?!"

"Rival prank," she answered through her teeth. "They do this before every game we play against them and I'm so tired of it. We prank them too, but, *ugh*, I *hate* when they play here. They always take it too far! Especially in the games before the championship tournament."

"How the hell...?" I looked at the arena. "How did they even get up that high to spray paint our backboards?"

"Didn't I just tell you they came here with their co-ed cheer squad?" Toni rolled her eyes. "They got one of their guys from their co-ed cheer squad and one of their girls to stand on the guy's shoulders to spray paint the words on the backboard. I caught them just as they got through with the last glass."

"But how did they get into our—"

Toni placed her hands on each of my shoulders. "No more questions, freshman. It's freezing out here and I'm in no mood to answer anymore of them. Plus, I'm way too pissed off." She sighed, peeking down at the red cups in my arms. "I'll explain inside. Put these cups back in your trunk. We gotta go scrub the backboards."

"We gotta go, what?!" I whined. "No way. Why? I've been out all night getting supplies. I am *done* and I want to do some underage drinking tonight to make up for spending my entire night getting this shit. Can't maintenance handle the cleanup in the morning?"

"They can." She walked off, blowing into her hands to warm them up. "But that's not BU school spirit. It's not what *we* do. We can't have our guys see that before the game. It'll fuck with their head. *Uh-uh*. We gotta fix it. Come on."

I shut my eyes tight and let my arms fall at my sides, dropping the cups to the floor.

"Fucking great."

"Still think you're *feelin'* Luke Lockett?" Toni taunted over her shoulder, closing in on the doors of our school building.

"Hell no!" I shouted back.

Because I thought nothing.

I knew it.

I knew I liked Luke.

I knew I liked him a lot.

And honestly? That was exactly where I went wrong first.

PART ONE

1st half...

"Love is a game because no matter how it ends, somebody always loses." - Unknown

NOW... FOR THE CULTURE MAGAZINE HQ, NEW YORK, NEW YORK – MONDAY, FEBRUARY 13, 2023

JULIETTE

MY BLACK DESIGNER heels clicked and clacked against the cement floors beneath me. En route to my editor-in-chief's office, I used the tip of my tongue to clean a few rice grains away from my gums.

Chinese food before 9am was probably not the best breakfast choice, but since I hadn't been to sleep in close to twenty-four hours, let's say my 9am wasn't exactly the 9am everyone else was having.

My editor-in-chief's office, constructed in four glass walls and a glass door, came into view the closer I walked.

She sent me an email marked *"urgent"* the moment she arrived in her office and I saw it immediately since I was already staring at my computer screen, typing.

I pulled an all-nighter the night before, completing work on two investigative pieces - one for our blog and the other set to go in our latest issue of For The Culture Magazine.

The last five years at For The Culture had been some of the best years in my journalism career. Then again, life at For The Culture was far more rewarding compared to my previous writing jobs at local newspapers where readers used our news articles for wrapping fragile items than for reading and enjoying.

My phone rang in my pocket and I quickly slid the device out of my white Harajuku joggers to see who was calling.

It was my cousin Sybil. Those of us who loved and knew her dearly referred to her as Billie, since she's always demanded we do so.

"What's up, Billie?" I asked, eyes connecting with my editor as I arrived steps in front of her glass door. "I'm heading into a meeting, so talk fast."

"Just calling to confirm champagne night at Pinkie's Champagne Bar later."

I rolled my eyes. "Why? So you know how much time you have left in the day to flake out on me?"

She sucked her teeth. "I'm not gonna flake. I'm excited about hanging out with my favorite cousin."

"Your *only* cousin... whom you *always* flake on."

"Oh, don't be like that, Juliette."

Mykal Jones, my editor, gestured for me to walk in and I held up a finger, signaling for her to give me a moment.

"Yes, champagne tonight at Pinkie's is a go," I told her. "And you better be there. I pulled an all-nighter at the office, so I need some bubbly in my system before midnight as a reset. So, don't play me out with your flaky ass."

"I'm there," she promised. "You can count on it."

No, I can't. Because she's about to flake out on me yet again.

My cousin loved the idea of going out with me more than actually doing it, but wasn't wise enough to know the reason she always canceled on me was because the only thing we had in common was that we were family. Though she was only a year older than me, my cousin and I were very different. Billie was comfortable in familiarity. I craved the unknown. She was more of a homebody. I loved getting lost in the city. She enjoyed watching movies at home. I preferred watching movies at the theater with friends. We were different, complete opposites, but the genuine love between us was our common ground.

And she was my *only* cousin.

We'd been doing this make-plans-to-go-out-and-she-cancel dance for several years because she always committed herself to going out with me, only to back out right before it was time to go.

I still loved her... but I'd be more shocked if she showed up instead of canceled on me, again.

"Gotta go," I announced, pushing my editor's glass door open. "Love you. See you tonight."

"Love you too and see you then," Billie replied, ending the call.

Once inside, Mykal's eyes did a quick appraisal of my thick copper curls shoveled into a messy top bun, my cognac chunky cardigan sweater, cropped white rib tank, and matching Harajuku joggers. Her eyes lingered on the black designer pumps on my feet.

Her brows furrowed next.

I pointed at her. "You made me promise to always arrive at our meetings wearing heels, so don't start."

"I told you to come to our meetings *polished* and with *heels* on, not mixing loungewear and pumps." She giggled. "This is a business casual getup I don't want to see again."

"I'm comfortable." I plopped down in the armchair across from her massive wooden desk. "And you're moving the carrot."

She waved her hand in the air. "I am not. I'm supposed to be mentoring you, Juliette, remember?"

Mykal was a fashionista to the bone. She loved fashion and wore everything like a model every day.

Me? I loved comfort. Give me a pair of high waist jeans and a thrift store tee and I'm ready any day.

I knew how to clean up well, though.

Nice little cocktail dress with designer heels to prove I cared about how I looked when I didn't.

Deciding what to wear was the least of my concerns when trying to break a story, anyway.

She twisted her lips to one side. "And correct me if I'm wrong, but didn't you have on this same thing yesterday? Minus the heels?"

I slid my hands into my pockets. "I did. I worked through the night."

"Juliette."

"Hey! At least I brushed my teeth, washed my face, and put on makeup in the bathroom this morning."

"Oh, God."

"What? I had the investigative piece on the gentrification of Brooklyn's Flatbush Ave due for the magazine and I had to do some last-minute research for the investigative report that I parred down for our blog."

She pursed her lips.

"I had to work. I had to get them done and I know my mentor isn't judging me for that since she used to do the same thing once upon a time."

"And why she's here to guide you and let you know it's unnecessary," Mykal insisted. "Desmond once told me work will always be work and life and a healthy mind is the real bag. And that changed *everything* for me."

I didn't like what she was telling me, but I couldn't help smiling as I watched her face light up just discussing her fiancé.

Her fiancé, Desmond Ellis III, proposed to her last summer, and she's been on cloud nine ever since. I couldn't wait to feel that rush of feelings. To being in that state of bliss and elation over romantic love. Just blushing at only the mention of my lover's name. But I was realistic. That day wasn't today. Because today, I understood that the feeling of seeing my byline in a magazine or on a popular blog offered a similar love high and at this point; I will take what I can get.

"After this meeting, go home." She instructed. "Eat some good food, get some quality rest, let your beautiful natural copper curls down, get some sun on your freckles and some color in your warm honey cheeks—"

"I had General Tso's and vegetable fried rice for breakfast and a large cup of black coffee with a shot of espresso the size of my head with no sugar, milk, or cream. I'm fed and so hopped up on caffeine, I won't sleep until next week." I pulled at the band around my thick copper curls, and my tresses fell past my ears and bounced on my shoulder blades. I shook my hair loose to release the rest of my corkscrew strands from the top of my head. "Curls? Down." I slapped the sides of my face a few times next. The sound of me doing so echoed around her chicly decorated office. "Is there color in my cheeks yet? If not, I can slap myself harder."

She snorted and held her hands up in front of her, surrendering to my antics.

"Okay." Mykal leaned back in her seat to cross her legs under her desk. "Fine. Since you're already in the no sleep, no play go-getter mindset, let's go. Let's do it. Because it's time." She smiled big, wiggling her brows.

I leaned in, curious.

"I've got the perfect piece that will show your range here at FTC and make you the *only* choice as editor-in-chief when I step down."

"Oh?" My brows piqued. "Tell me more."

Mykal had been with For The Culture since shortly after the magazine's launch in 2015. She was the cousin to one owner, Amir Jones, and has never let her familial tie dictate her move up in the magazine. Mykal went from intern to full-time employee, then to assistant editor to editor-in-chief in less than five years. I thought she was a rock star. A year younger than me, but with the drive of people several decades older, combined. She was a boss. Someone I'd grown to like more after Mykal met her fiancé Desmond, because she finally chilled out.

Desmond was once an editor at FTC too, before he left to start his own newspaper.

When Mykal tapped me on the shoulder one morning and asked to see me in her office during the fall of 2021, never did I imagine her saying she wanted to work with me to get editor-in-chief to prepare for her departure from FTC for Desmond's newspaper, The Ellis Daily. But I've followed her lead and built a trust in her, and her putting the idea of editor-in-chief in my mind has kept the EIC position in my crosshairs.

"So, what's the piece?"

"Sports," she chirped.

I dropped my back against the armchair I occupied. "Mykal."

"I know you've been avoiding writing sports pieces since you started here five years ago, but this is *the* one."

"Well." I blinked repeatedly, already annoyed. "What's the sports piece about?"

"More like *who*." She placed her elbows on her desk and balanced her face on the browns of her hands as if her face were the main course of the discussion. "Luke Lockett."

My first reaction to his name was to gag, and not intentionally. My stomach muscles literally tightened at the mention of his name, causing a wave of nausea to make me dry heave once. I slapped my hand to my mouth immediately.

"Whoa." She jerked her head back. "Okay, what the *hell* was that?"

The Chinese I had earlier and the coffee with espresso if I didn't swallow it all back down in time, is what that was.

I held my hand to my mouth, successfully keeping my unconventional breakfast in my stomach, and held up another hand in front of me, signaling for her to give me a moment.

Luke had been a constant discussion around the office and in the vast media since LU appointed him head coach at Langston University last summer. The youngest to hold the title of a head coach in Langston's collegiate basketball history, with experts predicting the

LU Blackbirds, would make it to the NCAA championships with Luke's coaching. He was a pop culture phenom in the making with a temper that didn't alarm, but that the female masses had deemed irresistibly sexy.

His latest on court outburst had gone viral last weekend after he got into an altercation with another coach at a game at Brookville University.

My alma mater.

I knew Mykal would want to do a story on him for FTC's upcoming issue. But because I never touched sports pieces since starting at the magazine in January 2018, I thought nothing of it. I knew I wouldn't be involved, so I didn't give a shit. But now...

"Uh-uh." I shook my head when I finally had the go ahead by my body's decision to keep my food in my stomach. "I'm not interested."

She blinked hard. "You're not interested in what?"

"In *anything* Luke Lockett."

"What part of *it is time* are you not understanding?"

I sighed, closing my eyes.

"*This* is what we've been discussing for the past year and a half, Juliette."

"I know."

"An article that is out of your usual scope that will show your ability to cover a range of topics. What an editor-in-chief should know how to do. You've worked on entertainment, fashion, beauty, and investigative pieces for our culture section, obviously. Now it's sports' turn, and this is the perfect piece. *What* is the problem?"

Luke is the problem.

He's my biggest problem.

"I just don't do sports," I claimed instead.

She squinted her eyes at me. "How do you know Luke Lockett?"

"*Hmm*?"

"Luke." She folded her arms over the lapels of her tailored brown blazer. "Why did you give the reaction you gave when I said his name? Do you know him personally? What's your history with him?"

He ruined me.

"*Is* there a history with him?" She arched a brow.

"No. Well. We... *shit.*" I pressed my fingertips to my eyes to soothe the sudden onset of a migraine. "Our alma maters are intrastate rivals, *so,* you know—"

"Oh, right!" She smiled bigger than before. "I *completely* forgot you went to Brookville. The beef between Brookville and Langston runs deep and for many, many decades."

I scoffed a laugh. "So deep, Brookville's faculty and upper-classmen teach all the incoming freshman at orientation that part of campus culture and life at BU is all about hating any and everyone from LU."

Mykal's humor at that echoed around us. "I always wished I went the university route so I could've experienced being petty for a reason. I would've been great at beefing with rivals."

Her comic relief made me laugh, and I was grateful for it.

"Well, shit." She fanned her hand in the air. "You graduated from BU almost twelve years ago. There's no way the rivalry runs that damn deep."

I shut my eyes. "Mykal."

"Juliette," she interjected in a stern tone. "I'm trying to say in the nicest, sweetest, most angelic way possible, to get the fuck over it."

I opened my eyes to see the serious expression on her face.

"After my and Desmond's wedding in August, I'm going to start my permanent move over to The Ellis Daily. Desmond wants me there full-time by the end of the year, and I want to be there even sooner than that. The semi-annual meeting with FTC's board is in June and I want you to do this piece so when I mention your name in that meeting when I announce my plans to resign, there will be no question who will get this office and this seat I'm sitting on."

I released a ragged exhale.

"Now I know all about busting my ass to get something and having that shit pulled from right underneath me. It doesn't feel good. And I'm not gonna allow that to happen to you and this editor-in-chief position." Mykal pointed at her chest. "I'm seeing to that."

She ran her fingers through her short hair.

"I don't understand." Mykal scooted forward in her chair, frustrated. "This is what we've been working on."

I nodded slowly.

"It *is* time, so." She leaned back in her seat again. "Whatever hang up you need to get over with Luke Lockett, do it quickly. Please. Like right now, because I'm setting up the interview for Wednesday."

"Wait, *this* Wednesday?"

"Yup."

I inhaled a deep breath. "Mykal, that's in only two days."

"It is. And I need the completed story by 7am Friday morning."

My eyes bulged.

"Luke will meet with our photographers on Friday afternoon. His story is the last write-up in this issue, which I'm now making our cover story."

"The cover story?!" I shrieked

"The cover story, Juliette."

Oh my goodness.

I brushed my palm slowly down my face, not caring about smearing my mascara.

This was moving way too fast!

"When I get your article," she continued, completely ignoring the look of horror on my face, "I'll send it over to our editors, proofreaders, and fact-checkers. In order to get our issue done on schedule, the digital printing press needs everything by Friday night, before midnight. And that's a deadline we must meet so we can go to print and I can have the first draft of our latest issue in my hands by the 28th."

"No pressure, right?"

"Pressure?!" She laughed. "This will be your easiest interview to date, I promise."

She has no idea.

"Plus, Luke Lockett is a single man who is super fine…"

And is.

"… brilliant and successful."

Extremely.

"And he's your first-class ticket to editor-in-chief before Christmas," she finished. "You're doing this interview and you'll do it well. Am I clear?"

"*Crystal* clear," I acknowledged begrudgingly. "Unfortunately."

* * *

Just as I knew she would do. Billie flaked on me.

Yet again.

She swore to me she was ready for a night at the champagne bar but a last-minute client at the beauty shop she works at, bursted through the doors with a hair emergency and Billie didn't have the heart to turn the woman away.

Billie's words.

Did it actually play out like that?

Time will tell, like always.

My cousin has a habit of exaggerating events. So I wouldn't consider her recent excuse for canceling our champagne plans to be any different.

My change in plans left me with nothing to do. My editor Mykal ordered me home, refusing to hear otherwise. With no champagne to sip or an office to be a workaholic in, my night was free. So, I decided I would entertain my friend with benefits, Blake, who was less benefits and even less than a friend. And me lying up under him trying to hold on to any sign of an orgasm as he pumped the last of his final deep strokes; I realized I was more of a benefit to him than he was to me.

It was quiet in my studio co-op. All 490 square feet of it. Wedged in between a 99¢ store and a boot camp gym, my over-priced co-op in a newly built two floor walkup on Flatbush Avenue was one result of the gentrification I've been researching in Brooklyn.

I angled my hips to receive Blake, whose rhythm of strokes was faltering. His breathing picked up speed as his hips struggled to carry out the rest of his actions.

I licked my lips and tried like hell to catch up. Rocking my hips in his erection's direction whenever he pulled back to thrust forward. My walls fluttered and my breathing hitched. I was *so* close.

But we were *so* damn quiet, and the silence was frustrating me and messing up my vibe.

It always bothered me, but never like tonight.

And to be clear, Blake was the quiet one. Not wanting to make the most of the noise, I suppressed my moans whenever I felt the urge to do it.

It was so silent between us, I could hear the B41 bus pulling up to the bus stop in front of my building from my opened window and also heard as people got on and off the bus.

Blake shuddered. My walls were fluttering, but more so from the friction and less because I was coming. Definitely not quivering strong enough to result in anything.

I was concentrating so hard on getting my nut my head was hurting.

Then, just like that... he was done.

Not catch his breath to get back into it *done*.

Finished *done*.

Another shudder and a flex in his biceps. The man climaxed and collapsed on top of me.

He laid on me for a few breaths.

Not wanting to be a bitch about it, I stroked his back with the tips of my pink, gel stiletto nails, bidding my time.

Really waiting for the right moment to request another round because the sex we just had could *not* be all he had to give. There was no way he was done, *done*.

He kissed my shoulder blade, then used his arms to push up and off me. I sighed at the sudden absence of his weight on me and watched the natural rise and fall of his ass as he walked away from my bed, then disappeared into my bathroom.

I pressed my head into my pillow and stared up at my ceiling, shaking my head.

Blake was a dating app find. My girls insisted I add the app, HeartMates, to my phone since they'd had some success with the app. None of them had started relationships, but they promised I would find someone who would at least be good company. My first date on the app was Blake. And that has been the only date we've been on since meeting up two years ago.

He was a nice guy. A resident doctor at Brooklyn Bay Medical Center a few miles from me. He studied pediatric surgery and his hours were unconventional, making him perfect for my schedule. We barely spoke on the phone. Only communicated through text conversations, often started by me, letting him know I was interested in hanging out if he was available.

My attention piqued at the sound of the faucet turning on in my bathroom sink.

He sure is taking a while to get back here.

Of course, we never actually hung out. Just fucked. And it was a toss-up he'd make me come when we did. Like literally, the brother was hella inconsistent in bed, which is why I continued to entertain him, even when he frustrated me. Because I convinced myself that when we met up, this would be the time he rocked me into a decent orgasm again, like the last time. But never a consistent dick appointment that left me satisfied. Because sometimes I'm happy. Other times disappointed. Tonight was feeling like another disappointing night.

Blake returned to the bed, still naked, dick flaccid and bouncing as he closed the space between us.

All that potential. Wasted.

I smiled at him. He reciprocated with a boyish grin. I turned to face him as he returned to my bed. I was more than ready to get back to it. So imagine my surprise when Blake gave me his back while pulling at my white down comforter to cover his naked body.

What the hell?!

I couldn't say what I was thinking. That would be too forward. So I scooted closer to him in bed, laid a hand on his forearm, and brought my lips to the nape of his neck.

He groaned at my touch and that did something to me. Something nice.

I kissed my way to his ear and whispered, "Can I get another round?"

He groaned again, this one not as erotic as the first groan.

"I'm a little tired," he explained. "Between pulling a twenty-eight-hour shift and still not recovering from a blind date over the weekend…"

I arched a brow.

"I'm beat." He repositioned himself onto his back to glance my way, then closed his eyes. "I think I'm gonna crash. Your bed is so comfortable."

I blinked a few times, trying to think of a nice way to say what I was about to say next, but there wasn't one.

"That's… flattering, I think." I told him as I balanced my weight on my hands to sit up. "And while I sympathize with you being tired, there's a more ideal place for you to *crash* and get some rest, Blake. *Your* place."

His eyes opened and locked with mine.

"Because I want to fuck *and* come."

He snorted.

"And in that *exact* order. You, however, seem to be done, so…" I popped my lips together. "That means it's time for you to go."

"Damn." He chuckled under his breath, displaying a dimpled smile. "It's like that, huh?"

I nodded slowly. "Definitely."

He laughed some more, which got a smile out of me.

The one thing I liked about Blake is he didn't take things too seriously. If it weren't for that one little thing that wasn't so little - his inability to prioritize my pleasure - I'd like him a little more.

"It's probably for the best, anyway," he agreed, lifting off my pillow and standing to his feet. I drew my heavy curtains open earlier, unintentionally giving people in a distance a view into my co-op. Blake clearly didn't care as he stood before me naked, dressing. "I've been getting kind of serious with someone else I've been seeing, another surgeon. She works at my hospital."

"Getting serious but still answering my "wyd" texts and going on blind dates with other people?"

He pushed his tongue into his cheek. "She and I haven't given each other labels or gotten physical yet..."

"Hey." I held a hand up to stop him. "It's cool."

And it was.

I mean, I'll admit. It stung a little; him mentioning seeing someone else seriously. But the glint in his eyes when he mentioned this other woman was cute. It didn't elicit thoughts of, *when will it be me?* Only reassurance that men were still catching feelings for women and making choices to be with them. They were still opening their hearts to the possibility of something permanent with someone and were interested in being *un*available.

It was refreshing and maybe a silly sense of relief, but to me, that little something meant something.

"Word of advice, though." I waited for his eyes to meet mine before I continued. "Make sure she comes first."

He tilted his head to one side.

"In bed." I blinked. "Give the girl a proper orgasm before you get yours. Women love that."

Blake pulled his shirt down over his head. "Are you trying to say you didn't come?"

"No."

"Oh," he exhaled.

"I'm not *trying* to say it. I'm *saying* I didn't." I bit at my bottom lip. "And the fact you had to ask should tell you I didn't. The body talks during sex. If I came, trust me, you'd know."

He laughed, running his fingers down his shaven chin. "Okay. That was very honest."

"Just looking out for the future *missus* in your life."

He smiled. "Okay, well, a word of advice for *you*?"

"Yes, please." I gestured for him to continue.

"Work less and let a man into your heart more."

I softened my eyes.

"Because truth be told, Juliette, I wouldn't have gone on any other dates if I felt my interest in you was being reciprocated." He arched a brow. "And that's real."

I scratched the back of my head. "Noted."

Would I let it ever happen? Probably not.

"You know," he started. "We could go again so you can get yours."

"Hmm..." I crossed my arms. "Now I'm too invested in the marriage I've created in my mind between you and your doctor bae. It's very Grey's Anatomy season one in my head right now."

He laughed.

"Don't jeopardize it, Blake," I advised. "If she's worth you ending things with me, then she's worth you going all in for."

Blake flashed a warm smile. "Well, this was the most amicable end of a fuck buddy relationship I've ever seen," he joked.

I snickered. "Agreed."

Blake left me with a kiss to my forehead, showing himself out shortly after, leaving me in bed alone with my thoughts.

Work less and let a man into my heart more.

The dangers in his innocent advice.

Because I almost did that once by mistake and I wasn't even in a relationship to get in that deep. But somehow I almost did. And thankfully, I smartened up quick before actually going through with it and suffering a devastating disappointment.

My device vibrated on my nightstand with a call. I palmed the device and slid it opened to answer when I saw it was my cousin.

"Yes, Billie."

"Oh my God, you sound pissed!"

I pursed my lips. "Well, if I sound it…"

"I apologize, Juliette. I was actually calling because I wanted to express how sorry I am again for missing champagne night at Pinkie's."

Under my breath, I snickered and rolled my eyes. "It's fine. I knew you'd cancel."

"Don't say that!" She sounded so offended. The dramatics. "I really had an emergency."

"I know, Billie." I shook my head. "Anyway, I found something else to do which ended up being a disappointment too, but at least the night wasn't a complete bust."

"*Awww*, Juliette."

"I needed the distraction, and it served its purpose, so it's fine."

"Distraction from what?"

I rolled onto my side in bed, my eyes drifting to my window. It was officially after 10pm, and you couldn't tell this with all the lights from businesses like restaurants and bodegas keeping the neighborhood lit. The gleams of light shined through my glass windows, lending light to my already lit co-op.

"My editor gave me my next assignment today, and it's giving me the blues."

"Why? What's the assignment?"

I inhaled a deep breath and released it slowly through my lips. "Interviewing Luke Lockett."

"That college basketball player turned basketball coach?! That's dope, Juliette!" she gushed. "He's a big deal right now, especially with talks that his team will do well in the NCAA championships."

"*Mm-hmm.*"

"Don't you two know each other, anyway?"

"Yup."

"He's the guy that gave you the ride back to campus your final year at BU, right?"

"*Uh-huh...*"

And I'll never forget it.

"... after you flaked on me back then as well, leaving me stranded in Manhattan." I ground my teeth back and forth. "Some things never change."

"Okay, for that? Leaving you in Manhattan like that? That was totally fucked up of me."

"With a capital F." I sucked my teeth, then giggled. "Been flaking on me for over twelve years. One thing you are, Billie, is consistent."

She laughed. "Stop!"

"Should've known your ways back then to save myself *a lot* of headaches."

"So what's the big deal, anyway? Why do you sound so down about it?"

Because I'm not ready to see him. I never wanted to see him again and even never was too soon.

"Don't tell me you're still committed to that BU - LU rivalry."

If only it was even that.

"I swear you all in that school of yours took your little back-and-forth beef way more seriously than y'all needed to," Billie continued. "I still think it was nothing but manipulation by those two universities."

"Anyway," I interrupted, desperate to escape the conversation. "I'm going to get some rest since I need it. I've been up for over twenty-four hours."

"Okay, cuz." She blew a kiss through the phone. "Call me tomorrow and we can see what plans we can arrange for the weekend."

"What? Girl, no." I scoffed. "I am too *done* with you this week."

"Juliette!"

"Let's try again next month, Billie."

She cackled. "Goodnight."

I told her I needed the rest, but I probably wouldn't get it. Not with Wednesday being so close. Because I was about to see the one man I believed ruined me in ways I haven't been able to recover from since I was 21-years-old. And I doubted the interview would make things any better.

I should've never accepted that ride home from him.

THEN... LANGSTON UNIVERSITY, NEW YORK, NEW YORK – SATURDAY, FEBRUARY 12, 2011

JULIETTE

DROVE ALL *this way to lose.*

It was game day at our rivals Langston University and I was amongst the few girls selected from our all-girl cheer squad to travel to the away game.

That didn't happen often. Neither BU's all-girl or co-ed cheer squads traveled much to conference games. This was the second year my coach selected me to travel in the four years I cheered for the school. Of course, I've traveled with the team to the championship tournament and an NCAA championship game. The only time I traveled to conference games hosted in other university arenas was my sophomore year, and this year, my final year at BU.

And both times were for games hosted at Langston University.

I guess because LU were our rivals, our athletics director made exceptions to have a BU cheer squad at LU to show school spirit. Plus, it was the first game of the season against LU.

The rivalry between Langston and Brookville was so deeply woven into the fabric of Brookville's academic identity.

The hate ran deep.

My cheer squad and I drove through miles and miles of traffic on a coach bus to get to LU.

Only to lose against them.

To say the loss annoyed me was an understatement.

"Where are the showers in here?" I asked, entering the women's basketball team locker room at Langston U's school arena.

"I think that way," my friend and fellow cheerleader, Clarke, answered, pointing to our right.

"Okay, cool." I spooled my copper curls into a compact bun, securing my hair in place at the crown of my head with a band. "I'm going to take a quick shower before heading out."

One of the few reasons I cared to drive out to LU was to watch the Ravens, LU's all-girl stomp and cheer squad. I was secretly obsessed with those girls and their dope ass cheer routines. I'd fangirl silently on the sidelines whenever they cheered for Langston during the few times the Ravens visited Brookville or when I visited LU with my cheer squad for an away game. Those girls made my all-girl cheer squad seem so lazy and dry at every rivalry game.

Where Brookville delivered in uniforms and campus beauty, Langston *always* had all the talent.

"Why don't you wait until we get back to Brookville?" Esme, another cheerleader and my friend, queried.

"She's not driving back with us," Clarke answered for me. "She's staying in the city with her cousin."

"Yup. What Clarke said." I smiled, grabbing my gym bag off the locker room bench. "I'm heading to the showers."

My other reason for caring to take part in cheering for Brookville at their first game that season against Langston was that I'd get to hang out with my cousin Billie in Manhattan afterwards.

She was from Brooklyn and still lived there with her mother. When I told her I would be in Manhattan for the game at Langston, she insisted I spend the weekend with her after the game ended and she'd drive me back to Brookville on Sunday night.

She didn't have to tell me twice.

I entered one stall in Langston's women's basketball team locker room. I would've hopped on the bus back to Brookville like Esme suggested without a shower, but I was going out with Billie and needed to freshen up.

The bathroom was vastly smaller than the locker room bathrooms at Brookville, but it was still clean. Plus, for what I had to do, the space was perfect.

With flip-flops on my feet, my bottle of body wash in one hand, and a netted bath sponge in the other, I entered one of the shower stalls. I dropped my towel on a hook behind the stall door and went straight for the shower's silver knob.

"Juliette," Clarke called the moment hot water sprayed from the shower head. "If you're all good heading out alone, we're going to leave to board the bus."

"Okay, I'm good," I confirmed, lathering my sponge with soap. "I'll see you tomorrow."

"Okay. And to be clear, you called your cousin Sybil, and she confirmed she'll meet you after the game, right?"

"Yeah." I ran the soapy netted sponge along my light brown limbs. "She didn't attend the game, but she told me she'd get me after."

"And coach knows?"

"I already spoke with her and she signed off on it before the game."

"Okay, and you're *sure* you're good, right? Your cousin will be here to pick you up?"

Members of my cheer squad knew how unreliable my cousin was and they'd never met her.

"*Yesss* Clarke," I replied, annoyed.

Thinking back on things, Clarke wasn't wrong to be concerned.

"Okay..." she acquiesced, walking out. "If anything changes, call me, all right? Have fun."

"Oh, I will." I giggled, soaping the last of my body parts with plans to stand beneath the spraying shower head.

And all was good for the next seven minutes. So good, I lathered up once again.

But that was a mistake because after that, the water just shut off.

Not trickled to a stop or gradually turned off.

The shower water shut off abruptly.

And I still had soap residue all over me.

This couldn't be happening.

Although Langston was no Brookville, I didn't doubt they paid their water bill.

I twisted the silver knob from left to right a few times to restart the flow of water, but nothing. So I quickly grabbed my towel to leave the stall and to check if the next one had water. There wasn't any water there either when I turned the silver knob.

There was no water coming from any of the stalls in that bathroom.

So there I was, in nothing but a towel. Soap residue so thick, tiny bubbles were popping on my skin as the soap dried with the air in the bathroom.

"What the hell?"

I took giant steps to the sink, reasoning I could use the sink's water to cleanse the rest of the soap off me. But no luck there either. No water flowed out of the faucet after I twisted the sink's knob.

My eyes connected with my freckled reflection in the mirror over the sink.

"Shit."

With no other choice, I ran my damp towel along my skin, doing my very best to get as much soap as I could from off my body.

"I'll have to shower again at Billie's," I mumbled as I wiped soap off my arms. "This is ridiculous."

The bottom of my bare heels stuck to my foam flip-flops as I walked my way to my gym bag I brought with me into the bathroom. Removing my change of clothes from the bag, I quickly stepped into my panties and snapped on my bra, then poked my head through the neck of my crew neck sweatshirt, cringing at how horrible my soapy skin felt against my team-branded sweatsuit.

"This night is starting off well."

Fully dressed, I pulled my phone out of my bag to see another issue. My battery was at three percent.

My heart practically dropped.

I'll admit. I liked to live my life a little on the wild side and procrastinated terribly back then. Sometimes that included failing to charge my phone whenever I had the opportunity. I also always forgot to keep a charging wire on me. It wasn't uncommon for me to think I could borrow a charger and charge my phone anywhere.

Langston U's locker room bathroom was not the *anywhere* I had in mind, and I was now by myself in that bathroom with no one to ask for a charging wire.

I used my minimal phone battery life to call Billie and let her know I was heading out and for her to pick me up in front of the school, because I probably wouldn't have time to call again.

"Hello?" she answered on the third ring.

Hip hop music blasted in the call's background, and I smiled with excitement.

"Hey girl, I'm ready when you are!" I shoved my towel into my bag. "And I have little battery life on my phone. So, hurry and get here—"

"Oh my God, Juliette," she started, and I already didn't like her choice of words or the tone in her voice. "I'm so sorry! My girl Arabella pushed me into a car and told me we're going to a basement party in Jersey. So that's where I'm going right now."

"Excuse me?!" I yelled, because there was no way I could ask any other way.

"I won't be able to pick you up," she hollered over the music. "I don't even have my car."

"Billie." I took a breath to calm my panicked heart. "Are you fucking with me? Tell me you're fucking with me."

"No." She giggled, not understanding the severity of the situation. "I'm serious! Arabella gave me no other choice."

She was always so unnecessarily dramatic.

"Girl, what the fu—" My hand went to my chest. Billie left me feeling pissed and distraught, and I couldn't decide what to feel more. "So... are you *saying* she kidnapped you?" My voice echoed around the bathroom. "Is *that* what you're saying?"

"Well, no, not *kidnapped*."

"Fuck, Billie," I exhaled. "What the hell am I supposed to do now? My team told me they were leaving—"

"You better run and get on that bus, cuz!" she advised. "Because we're already driving through the Holland Tunnel."

I gasped. "Bitch!"

"I'm so sorry," she apologized. "I'll call you later. I love you."

And with that, she ended the call.

"Oh my God," I whispered.

With no opportunity to think, I just acted. A second later, I was stuffing the rest of my stuff into my bag, including my hooded puffer coat, and booking my way toward the locker room's exit.

I didn't bother changing into my sneakers. I had to run in flip-flops.

There was no time.

With luck, my cheer squad was still boarding the bus and I could at least catch up to them as the driver was starting the engine.

Out of the arena and through the public entry lobby, I charged through Langston's shiny glass turnstile doors to get outside to see the parking spot where our bus parked earlier, empty.

I wanted to faint.

A moonlit night with specs of light from the surrounding campus buildings, traffic lights, and crosswalk signals was the only thing waiting for me on the other side of those turnstile doors.

I pushed my shaky hand into my bag in search of my phone and yanked out my device to call Clarke.

But that was worthless because the moment I clicked the top button to wake my phone up, nothing happened.

My phone had turned off. The battery was dead.

"Damn," I heard expressed feet away from me.

I twisted quickly to find *the* last person I wanted to see while dealing with a crisis.

"Your team ain't give a fuck about you, huh?"

I rolled my eyes closed and grunted to myself.

Besides being outside in close to twenty-degree weather with no jacket on, flip-flops on my feet, and only wearing my losing school team branded sweatsuit feeling every bit of that New York City cold air, Luke Lockett was there to see me at probably one of my lowest moments.

Fucking great.

"Don't start with me," I fumed.

"And where are your shoes, shorty?" Luke quizzed next.

"Didn't I tell you not to start with me?!" I yelled at him. "I'm not in the mood."

He held his hands up defensively.

To make matters worse, Luke was fresh faced and bright eyed as if he'd just gotten up from the best beauty rest refreshed and not like he just finished playing a game against my school, kicking our asses mercilessly.

The loss was an embarrassment. An 84-38 loss. The college basketball commentators would be dragging our school by Monday.

Brookville had one more game against Langston in March the following month. But the way Brookville's basketball team performed that night on LU's court, I was positive we'd lose the next game, too.

I dropped my view to my phone again, clicking the hell out of the top power button, hoping the phone would grow a heart quick enough to have mercy on me and power back on.

It didn't. Only gave me the picture of a low battery on the black screen.

I dropped my head back between my shoulders. "This is not happening."

"Here." He walked up to me. Luke towered over my 5'5 height comfortably. I had to calm my heart from feeling anything when he approached.

Since literally running into him my freshman year all those years ago, I've had to calm my excited heart a lot whenever I saw him. Even though the most words we'd ever exchanged were that night after the game, standing outside of his school at LU. He was collegiate famous. A live wire but loved by everyone. Well, everyone outside of Brookville U. So, it wasn't hard for me to remember I wasn't supposed to like him. Brookville had conditioned me long enough because of my affiliation with Brookville to repel any semblance of interest in Luke Lockett or anything associated with Langston University.

But it would probably take mind control technology to get me not to feel anything for either of the aforementioned.

Luke extended his arm toward me with his phone in hand. The sleek device's back light lit up under the night sky. "You can use my phone to call whoever."

His voice was *so* perfect. Deep, raspy, easygoing, and so damn unfair for a guy to have. Especially when that guy only turned 21-years-old two months prior. I hated I knew that about him. Hated his voice had the effect it had on me and that I noticed it at all.

"I don't know anyone's number," I admitted.

He arched a bushy brow.

"I save everyone's number under their name. I don't know anyone's phone number by heart except for my parents, but they live deep in Long Island."

"Damn." He pulled his hand back with the phone, dropping the device into his back jeans pocket. His beautiful brown eyes focused out into the distance, staring off as if in thought. For New York City, the block the university occupied and the close surrounding area was quiet.

I pressed my hand to my forehead and sighed.

"I'll drive you back."

"What?"

He sucked his teeth. "Man, don't make me repeat myself."

I stared at him for a moment, choosing to focus on thick lips and perfectly trimmed facial hair.

"No." I pressed my lips together. "I'm good."

"You're actually *not* good, suburban girl." He insisted. "Not out in this brick ass cold in flip-flops, without a coat, and with no other way to get back on campus. Be real with yourself."

I narrowed my eyes at him.

"Aight, look, check it." He clapped his hands once, then gestured at me with prayer hands. "The *only* reason I'm offering to drop your stubborn butt back to your wack ass campus is because I got three older sisters and I would hate the dude who had the means to help one of them but didn't all because of some petty shit he was on." He lifted and dropped his broad shoulders in his down jacket. "So what's up, suburban girl?"

I swallowed hard, turning to squint in the direction I remember the bus driving in from when we arrived at LU hours ago. I don't know what I was searching for. Maybe the bus's tail-lights, so I'd have some kind of hope of not having to share space with Luke.

Not that the idea itself didn't excite me a little.

"No," I shook my head. "I'd rather walk all the way back to Brookville."

The bite of cold air against my bare feet let me know they'd be ashy blocks of ice before I reached the end of the block if I made good on my word.

I was buggin'.

Luke shrugged and flashed that sexy dimpled grin of his that earned him the nickname LL, like the rapper, in and out of Langston.

"Suit yourself, baby," he remarked, backing away. "Make sure you check the MTA bus schedule on your phone to see when the next one arrives so you can stand at the bus stop in time to take it to the subway, then the LIRR. Oh, that's right." He pointed at the phone in my hand. "Your phone is dead."

I kissed my teeth.

"I hope you know Morse Code, shorty." He chuckled, pointing over his shoulder at the dorms. "I'mma head back to my room and get some rest. I came out here to grab a slice from the pizzeria a few blocks up, but I'm exhausted after whopping your boys' asses tonight."

"Fuck," I gritted.

I would've been a prideful idiot and a complete dummy if I didn't take Luke up on his offer.

And my parents didn't raise a fool.

"Okay," I shouted. "All right. I accept your offer to drive me back. Thank you."

I mumbled the last sentence. The one containing my gratitude. It just hurt so much to say it out loud.

"I'm sorry? I didn't hear that last part." He framed his ear with his big hand and turned his ear my way. "What was that *last* thing you said?"

I balled my hands into a fist and repeated through my teeth, "Thank you."

* * *

We were quiet for the first nine minutes of the ride. I had the perfect distraction, too.

A view of New York City at night.

Billie may have robbed me of the opportunity to spend a night out in the city with her bullshit, but at least I could sightsee the

Empire State Building and all the lights from Manhattan's nightlife as we made our way through traffic to get to the interstate.

Luke's silver Honda looked better than I was expecting. Not that I was expecting LU's star shooting guard to drive a death trap or anything. I just didn't expect to be so comfortable riding beside him. Inside smelled of black vanilla because of the air freshener shaped like a tree swinging off his rearview mirror by a springy string. Miguel's "Sure Thing" played from the car's speakers at a comfortable level.

I didn't focus my attention on him for the first nine minutes sitting as a passenger in his car. But at the nine-minute mark, I built up the courage to take glimpses of him in the driver's seat from the side of my eyes.

He bobbed his head to the r&b playlist of music playing, with one hand on the steering wheel the other stroking his goatee, in his own zone, I guess. His disposition was super chilled and cool. Like nothing could knock him off his block. It was easy to feel comfortable in his company.

At that moment, I understood the allure.

Understood it completely.

Honestly, it was never a mystery to me, either.

And that was frustrating.

"Thank you, again, for doing this," I said, finally breaking the silence between us.

He glanced at me for only a second before returning his attention to the road ahead. "You're welcome."

Silence again.

"Yo, what's your name?" He asked.

I turned my head to look at him.

"I only realized after we got in my car that I don't even know your name."

"So that's why you keep referring to me as *shorty, baby,* and *suburban girl?*"

"Yes, and no." He smiled to himself. "You look like a *shorty,* a *baby,* and a *suburban girl* to me."

That stung a little. I mean, obviously there wasn't really an opportunity for my name to precede me. I wasn't a basketball player at BU. I wasn't even the head cheerleader of my cheer squad.

But... I don't know.

I guess because I knew his name; I figured he knew mine, too.

Or at least I hoped.

"Juliette."

He made a shrugging motion with the sides of his mouth and repeated, "Juliette."

Hearing my name roll off his tongue and spoken in his voice made me inhale a lung full of air.

It sounded so right coming from his lips.

"Juliette," he voiced again. "Why didn't you change into your sneakers or something before getting in the car? Your feet don't get cold?"

I peeked down at the floor of his car at my feet, wiggling my toes in my flip-flops, feeling the soap residue between them.

"The water shut off while I was trying to take a shower in your women's basketball team locker room, so I'm covered in soap. Especially my feet."

He snorted, folding his lips into his mouth.

"What's so funny?"

He shook his head, swallowing the rest of his humor, I guess. "Rival prank."

I wrinkled my brows.

"The team shut the waters off for BU's basketball team. I didn't think they would do it to y'all too."

I twisted in my seat to face him. "Are you kidding me?!"

"Aye," he started. "Don't get loud with me. I didn't do it."

I twisted forward in my seat again, gritting my teeth.

The rival pranks were the most exhausting thing about playing against Langston U. Even more than losing against them. Whether our game was home at Brookville or in the city at Langston, they always pranked us. And we always had to return the favor, continuing the vicious cycle of pranks yearly.

My first year at BU, it was LU's basketball team and co-ed cheer squad spray painting the backboards of which took my cheer squad hours to clean up. We didn't have our pre-game party that night because we were so tired after exerting all that energy. The year after that, when Langston U played Brookville U for their first game of the season, every time my cheer squad stood to do a cheer, LU's school band played BU's school song devastatingly off-key and loudly irritating the shit out of all of us.

Langston did not play coy or fair with their pranks. And they were quite creative, knowing just how to get underneath our skins.

I probably would have left this latest prank alone and not continued to address it, but Luke kept snorting and failing to hold back his laugh behind his steering wheel and that made me want to punch him in his perfect mouth.

"I find nothing funny about this." I turned to face him in my seat. "My skin is itching and I'm literally *dying* in reaction to this feeling of my skin crawling."

He glanced again, smirking, and quipped, "You'll be aight."

"Fucking asshole," I retorted. A total knee-jerk reaction. I never knew how to keep being angry to myself.

He looked over at me again and scoffed a laugh. "If I was such a *fucking asshole*, I would've left you standing outside of LU, continuing to look lost and confused."

"I wasn't lost *or* confused," I clarified. "I was *pissed* and you're pissing me off more."

"Oh, *I'm* pissing *you* off? I didn't leave you behind," he reminded. "Your team did that."

He leaned forward in his seat to check over his left shoulder and stepped more on the gas, picking up speed to match the flow of traffic as we merged into traffic on the interstate.

"My team didn't leave me," I spat. "I had plans to spend time in the city with my cousin, but she didn't show up."

"Damn, so even worse?" he started. "Your own family bailed on you?"

"You are so damn insensitive." I jabbed my finger in his direction. "You and your stupid ass team. Like? Who turns the water off on people?"

"Don't get all high and mighty because your wack student body can't put your bougie ass brains together long enough to come up with a better prank."

Oop! Burn.

"The problem is y'all have too much damn cash to play with over there."

I rolled my eyes.

"Y'all would much rather spend mad money on a sky writer to leave taunts along the sky over LU or get an expensive ass brander to brand your team's logo on our front lawn." He laughed. "You think that shit bothers us? We think it's cute. We're flattered y'all would splurge on a prank and it has no effect on us."

"Shut up."

Honestly, I didn't care. Luke could've dragged every person who called Brookville home at my school and I wouldn't blink an eye. I didn't love Brookville the way other students at the university loved it. Didn't even like it. And since it was my final year, and I still had developed no undying Brookville Lions pride, I was pretty sure I never would.

"I hate you," tumbled out my mouth, though. "I hate you and your stupid school."

No, I didn't.

"You all are so *damn* annoying," I added, because that was the only true thing. "Who the hell cares *that* much about fucking basket-ball, anyway? God."

"Well, shit, I hate Brookville and everything your school stands for, so I guess I hate your ass, too. We even."

I stared ahead of me, my eyes focusing on the yellow deer crossing sign on the side of the road until we passed it. I rolled my tongue in my mouth, fighting the feeling of wanting to scream and cry. Not at his words, but that I cared he had the gal to speak them out loud to me.

"Your jump shots suck," I spat. "With your *lanky* ass."

"And you just *suck*, period, as a cheerleader," Luke fired back. "I didn't even know your name... with your *fat* ass."

My jaw dropped.

"Cheer squad lame as fuck. The lamest I've ever seen and I've seen plenty," he continued, not batting an eye. "I don't get it. Why do y'all show up on the sidelines to do nothing? Beauty can take you, but so far."

I whipped my head in his direction, and he met my glare. Face to face and sitting less than an arm's reach away from each other allowed me to get an unobstructed view of *the* Luke Lockett. Star shooting guard of the acclaimed Langston University Blackbirds. With the gentlest eyes and sexiest natural, up-turned lip corners at the sides of his mouth.

And his lips...

They were so full and shaped like a perfect bow. A girl could lose track of time kissing him, and not care, I was sure.

We were only eyeing one another for less than a second when I snatched my attention off him to peer forward again. More so to gain control over my breathing since I'd held onto my inhale the moment we locked eyes.

Thinking I'd only see an empty road ahead with taillights in the distance, my eyes ballooned when they landed on a dead deer's carcass in the middle of the interstate and Luke's wheels aligned perfectly to collide with it.

I gasped.

"Oh, shit!" Luke perked up in the driver's seat immediately.

He glanced at the rearview mirror quickly, then the passenger side mirror, pumping the brakes while twisting the steering wheel to the right to move out of the path of the deer. But it must've been too late. Because a moment later, the car's front wheels ran over the deer, causing his Honda to tilt to its right for a beat, then skid a little on the road.

I screamed, slapping my hand over my mouth to muffle the noise.

Luke remained silent, holding tight to the steering wheel and twisting it from left to right to gain control of the car.

I grabbed the left side of my seat and squeezed until my nails ached. Shut my eyes and held my lids tightly closed, listening to the tires screech against the road. I believed we were about to crash into something. I only opened my eyes when I felt the car come to a gradual stop.

My breathing was ragged as I opened my eyes to nothing but road up ahead. We were fine, the car a little worse for wear, I was sure. Luke had brought the car to a stop safely on the shoulder of the interstate and out of the way of traffic. Thankfully, we didn't get stopped by a tree like I imagined happening the moment he tried to regain control of his car.

I pressed my hand to my chest, feeling my heart hammer against it. I tried like hell to get hold of myself.

Luke placed a warm hand on my hand closest to him that gripped the side of his passenger seat. I peeked down at his hand on mine and lifted my gaze to him.

"You aight?" He asked, chest heaving up and down as he leaned forward to search my eyes for the answer. "You good?"

"Yeah," I whispered, and corroborated with a nod. "Yes. Are you?"

He nodded too, moving his hand off me and to the ignition to turn off the car. His other hand was at his door handle, opening his door a second later.

I'd only placed my hand on my door handle when he ordered me to, "Stay in the car, Juliette. Do not get out," before leaving the vehicle.

I watched him through the front and back windshields as Luke checked around his car.

He grabbed the top of his head with both hands as he stared down at his left front tire.

"Shit." I dropped my head against the headrest and shut my eyes. "Could this night get any worse?"

Luke returned to the car, dropping himself into his seat and immediately reaching for his phone that was inside of his cup holder.

"It's a flat," he announced. "A *terrible* flat. I think the deer's antlers pierced right through my front tire. Shit."

"The antlers? How do you know that? Are the antlers still attached?" I turned in my seat to check if I could see the deer through the back windshield. "Did we drag that thing with us?"

Luke twisted his head to focus my way and busted up laughing, holding his fist to his lips. "*That's* what you're worried about?"

I rolled my eyes away.

"I'll search up a tow truck company," he suggested through his laughing. "Hopefully they can repair it right here and we can continue on to Brookville."

* * *

To answer my question - yes, the night could get worse. Stranded in the middle of nowhere overnight, kind of worse, actually.

Kaysville was the name of the town. It looked like it was in the middle of being renovated, as told by the newly developed infrastructure, awkwardly placed here and there. Some patches of area had fancy buildings with glass balconies. Other areas had properties with shuttered windows and missing cement staircases. Near the end of the town, the city line, a mile before crossing into a neighboring village, abandoned houses, and a motel took up space along the strip of land along the interstate.

Luke and I had no choice but to check into that motel.

"The good news is, this is a simple fix," the aging mechanic told us shortly after his arrival and following a quick examination of what Luke had diagnosed as a flat.

Luke used our location and Google to find a tow service and happened upon Kaysville Car Tow as the first listing, which showed the car tow company was also a mechanic shop and scheduled to close in five minutes.

"The bad news is," the mechanic added, "it isn't only a flat. You've got some grease leaking underneath your car, which might mean you've got some damage to one of your axel components. This may mean your front wheel drive axel got damaged and will need to be replaced. I'd have to bring it to my shop to confirm."

At Luke's orders, I remained in the car listening to him and the mechanic speak through the lowered passenger side window. I only obeyed because I was partially to blame for the situation.

"Now I got the tools to change both the tire and the axel, but my shop is closed for the night and I gotta make it home to my ol' lady. I'm already late for dinner." The mechanic glanced at the car. "And I wouldn't advise you to drive this car anywhere tonight because you'd be going nowhere extremely fast."

"Shit," I whispered.

"So, what are we supposed to do?" Luke asked, folding his arms over his chest.

The mechanic arched a salt and pepper brow.

"Sir," Luke added. "What are we supposed to do, sir?"

The mechanic half smiled. "Better."

Luke smiled back. "My apologies for my tone, but, like, are we supposed to sleep on the side of this road tonight?"

"Of course not." He chuckled. "You two will ride in my tow truck cab and I'll tow your car. I own the motel next to my shop and can put you and your girlfriend up for the night. No extra charge."

"She's not my girlfriend," Luke corrected.

Because that needed to be explained.

I shook my head at my annoyance with it.

"Okay, all right." He glanced my way. "Your friend then."

"She ain't that either."

I stuck my head out of the passenger window. "Will you shut the hell up and let this man help us? God. So damn petty."

The mechanic laughed under his breath. "I can work on your car first thing in the morning before daybreak. By the time you two wake in the morning, your car will be ready."

Wake in the morning?

That was funny.

Because besides being stuck with the likes of Luke for longer than originally planned, once I laid eyes on the comped motel room in Kaysville after we left Luke's car with the mechanic at the mechanic's auto shop next door to the motel, sleep was the last thing I wanted to do.

It was like I stepped into the 20th century. At first glance, the only thing that appeared new in the motel room was *us*.

Honestly, the only thing that kept me from thinking our lives were in danger was me remembering the sweet, down-home nature of our mechanic. Because the motel room was creepy as fuck.

The old-fashioned bedding was the first thing my eyes fell on. The bed, though huge, had the ugliest floral bedding I'd ever seen on a bed. And I wish I were exaggerating.

I *really* do.

But nothing could compete with the green and white patterned carpet covering the floors. The smell of old wood was thick in that room, and I mean *thick*. I was practically getting splinters inhaling the surrounding air. And the stench was probably coming from the old ass dresser and side tables that, although they were in good condition, had pulls that looked older than my parents.

"This place is... interesting," I commented, eyes still scanning the room.

Luke walked past me, shrugging off his down coat. "Looks fine to me."

"*This* looks fine to you?" I asked, dropping my bag on the aged ottoman. "Looks like a scene out of the old horror film *'Bates Motel'* to *me*."

"Those of us who aren't used to living in mansions can appreciate a decent place to lay our heads," he snarled, checking around the room. "The mechanic is allowing us to stay here for free. Be grateful."

I whipped my head in his direction. "I *am* grateful. Pointing out the obvious, that the room looks *interesting* to put it nicely, is not indicative of me being *un*grateful, so calm down." I folded my arms next. "And *who's* used to living in mansions, exactly?"

He shot me an exaggerated stare.

I had to laugh at that. "*You* think *I* live in a mansion?"

"So you about to play dumb in my face and pretend like all of you who go to Brookville don't come from a certain class?"

"Working class?" I challenged. "Because that's the class I'm from."

He made a sputtering sound with his mouth. "Yeah, aight."

"I mean, yes." I caved. "Does most of Brookville's student body come from households with parents who fall into a certain tax bracket? Yes." I shrugged. "So I can see where your confusion is coming from. But *my* parents actually work for their money."

"Oh yeah?" He folded his arms over his chest. "For who and doing what?"

I cleared my throat.

"Huh?" Luke pushed.

"They... they work for themselves and own a laundromat."

He arched a brow. "Only one?"

"Four."

"And that's it?" He asked. "Just laundromats?"

I pushed my tongue into my cheek and answered, "And two organic dry cleaners."

"Organic." He chuckled to himself. "Working class, my ass."

"Whatever. I don't have to prove shit to you." I snatched up my bag. "I'm going to take a shower and get all this old soap off my body."

"Have fun," he taunted.

I was feet away from the door when I realized, "Damn. There is nothing in here for me to sleep in. "I peeked in my bag. "Okay, I see my varsity shorts—"

"Here." He pulled at the hem of his sweater, taking it off to reveal a white tee underneath. The tee was next to come off and once he held it out in his hand in my direction, he demanded I, "Take it, it's clean."

My eyes rolled down to his bare chest. His pec muscles firm. Arms lean, long and defined. His skin was as dark and obsidian clear as his face. I had to force my eyes off his narrowed waist.

"I put it on ten minutes before running into you outside my school, but before that, it came out of a laundry bag."

My eyes bounced from the shirt to his eyes.

"Take it," he directed again.

I took the shirt and said, "Thank you," walking the shirt and my bag to the bathroom.

In an odd discovery, the bathroom wasn't as old fashioned as the rest of the motel room.

It was like the motel's interior decorator cut, copied, and pasted the bathroom into the motel room. The amenities matched nothing outside of the bathroom's doors. Natural stone vanity counter with his and hers basin sinks. A stall shower with two shiny silver detachable shower heads. Glossy faux marble floors.

Like, what?!

I was so thankful for the opportunity to cleanse my skin. I didn't bother to give the mismatched old fashion and modern design another thought and simply got underneath the shower. My day had been one I would've never imagined. With everything that transpired starting with my phone call with Billie, I hadn't had time to consider how insane the past two hours had been. It hadn't seemed like only two hours.

Finally, being able to take a normal shower with my body wash, bath sponge, and to dry off with the motel's fresh towels when done, I could acknowledge and appreciate how much of a blessing Luke had been in this situation. My night could've gone a completely different way. Worse than I probably would've imagined.

Out of the shower and moisturized with the bottle of lotion I kept in my gym bag, I stood over the bathroom's vanity, inhaling Luke's shirt before poking my head through the neck hole.

There were traces of his natural scent mixed in with the light fragrant detergent whoever washed his clothes used. That simple detail proved someone genuinely adored Luke and took good care of him.

And maybe, just *maybe,* he wasn't *so* bad because of that.

Dressed in Luke's white tee that fit me perfectly and my red varsity shorts with the Brookville Lion's team logo on the right side, I redid my copper top bun and stepped out of the bathroom, reentering the room.

Luke unwound on the side of the bed closest to the bathroom, brushing his smooth waves towards his forehead with the soft bristles on a mini double-sided soft-hard brush.

He glanced my way and paused, brushing for only a second before resuming and meeting my eyes. "Better now?"

"Yes." I dropped my bag to the right of the bathroom's door. "*Much* better."

"Cool."

"So." I glanced over his shoulder at the bed. "We need to address the *one bed* situation."

Luke quit brushing his hair this time to straighten his back in his seat on the bed. "I wasn't aware there was a situation."

"There's only one bed and two of us."

He turned to examine the bed like he hadn't been sitting on it that whole time. "It's a gigantic bed. You can sleep on one side and I'll sleep on the other."

"Oh, uh-uh." I frowned. "I'm not sharing a bed with you."

"Oh?" He looked me right in my eyes and said, "You don't plan to sleep tonight?"

I folded my arms.

"Because *I* do." He watched as I pressed my back to the popcorn wall behind me. "I already told you I was tired after the game tonight. I didn't ride that bench, not once. But I didn't want to leave you out in front of Langston all by yourself."

I twisted my lips to one side.

"Now, I done drove you all the way out here and we're still only sixteen miles away from your school. A school I *really* don't like." He held up his fingers to count on them. "So now I'm tired, annoyed, and my car got fucked up, which I must pay for. I ain't hear you offer to help with that, or at the very least give me gas money. Not once."

I parted my lips to defend myself.

"And I ain't asking you for a dime," he interjected. "Trust me, I got it. But what I don't got is the patience to tolerate the new bullshit you coming at me with. Because what you're not gonna do? Is tell me I can't sleep in this old ass rickety bed for whatever reason you wanna give."

Luke looked me up and down, taking in his crisp white tee I wore that hung over my varsity shorts. Shorts that hugged my full hips and round thighs. "You ain't gotta worry about me. You are good. I already told you I got three big sisters, a mama and a pops. They've all taught me how to keep my hands to myself and my ass out of trouble. I know how to respect boundaries. So don't even trip."

I was really about to sleep in a bed with a guy I've only got close to hours prior.

"Well, good. Because you better not touch me," I told him.

He laughed. "If you don't want me to touch you, I won't touch you, shorty."

"Good."

"Great." He gestured with the tiny brush at my breasts. "But judging by how hard your headlights are beaming in my white tee..."

I scoffed, folding my arms over my chest.

"...I'm thinking you want me to do more than touch, but it's your world, *Juliette*. Whatever you want, you got it."

"My nipples are hard when it's cold."

"But it ain't cold in here." He smirked. "So why are they so hard right now?"

Luke always had an arrogant vibe to him, which made it easy not to like him. And while his annoying personality traits should've been a turn-off, it was doing quite the opposite to me that night.

"Even if I *wanted* to..."

Which I did.

"I'd break you, Luke," I voiced confidently. "Snap you in two. I'm way too much for you."

"I bet you wouldn't." His eyes glided up the curves on my frame. "'Cause if your comment is about your weight, I've had way thicker, and they weren't the ones doing the breaking." He shrugged. "You're just really bottom heavy, if anything. Pear-shaped. You'd be nothing but light work for me."

"You called me fat."

"I said *with* your fat *ass*." He dropped his head back a little to view me through low lids. "'Cause you got a lot of ass and it's fat... suburban girl."

Luke licked his lips slowly, visually digesting my body, and his attention was doing things to me.

"I bet you wouldn't last over five minutes."

He smirked. "Bet I'll last the entire night."

Sounds of cars whizzing down the interstate outside the motel room's door filled the silence between us.

What the hell was I doing?

Finding some relief from my stressful ass night is what.

I rubbed my lips together and dropped my eyes to the crotch of his jeans. Noticing where my attention drifted, Luke grabbed himself in front of me and, for some sadistic reason, his doing so made me smile.

"I bet your dick is tiny."

He swiped his tongue along his bottom lip. "Bet you can't take it all."

Was the shift in our night random? Maybe. It was definitely unplanned. But there was something about Luke Lockett that drew me to his brazenness, something that made me want to shut him up.

And to finally explore him, if I'm being honest.

It was my last year at Brookville and his last year at Langston. I reasoned the game we had against Langston the next month would be the last time I ever saw Luke in person again. Since my freshman year, I have been curious about this six-foot-something guy from Brooklyn. I'd be a fool to leave our time together without something to remember it by. Plus, my day was hella shitty.

I deserved whatever it was I got tonight, and with hope, it was something good.

"I bet I won't even come," I protested low.

Luke left his seat at the edge of the bed, tossing the brush on the nearest side table. He closed the distance between us. Pressed his palms flat against the rough wall behind me and leaned in real close to whisper in my face. "I bet you'll come first, *Juliette*."

My name on his lips and those lips positioned only inches from mine was all the motivation I needed to move the other half of the way and to balance myself on the arches of my feet to kiss him.

Our lips touched, and there was a spark between us. Literal static that shocked us at the same time. But it didn't stop us. It took only one peck of our lips before he went searching for my tongue with his. The kiss had heat. And aggression. It was us wanting to dominate and refusing to relinquish control to the other. A sensual sword fight with heavy breathing and moans rooted in sexual frustration. I tried to keep my eyes open, but the guy was kissing me too good. His hands left his sides and began palming my ass in my shorts, using his grip on me to bring me closer to him and on my toes. Soon he moved one of those hands between us, sliding his long fingers into the top band of those varsity shorts, then between my thighs to find no panties but a lot of wetness.

He chuckled on my lips, arrogantly of course, before breaking our kiss. I opened my eyes to his.

"Talking 'bout you hate me." He grinned and circled my clit with his middle finger. "But you're wet for me like this."

I gritted my teeth in response and shoved him away from me.

He laughed.

"You're such a fucking jerk," I sneered. "My goodness!"

He bit his bottom lip and grabbed his hard-on through his jeans. "A fuckin' jerk who you want to fuck you good though, right, *Juliette?*"

Right.

I pulled his shirt I wore up and over my head, then removed my shorts next. I stood before him for two whole seconds, maybe three, wearing nothing but confidence. His eyes dropped below my neck and he licked his lips while approaching again. Luke bent his tall frame at the knees and picked me up, turning to the bed.

"Yeah," he slapped my ass as he carried me that way. "That's what I thought."

While the room smelled of old wood, the bed smelled like fresh linen. And in the few seconds I laid there waiting for Luke to sheath his erection with the condom he slid out of his wallet, I cringed, wondering how many other people laid beneath these covers like this.

Luke didn't leave me alone long enough to let my mind wander. Because soon after he climbed into bed, he got in position on top of me. Pushing my legs back using the back of my thighs. Rubbing his hard against my soft, real slow. Then slid in even slower, adamant about giving me every inch of his dick that *wasn't* small at all.

I could take it though... I think.

His girth stretched my walls, and I sighed at the pressure Luke applied with each thrust forward.

He dropped his head to his chest as he held himself up with straight, lean, muscular arms. I watched him struggle at first to compose himself with the first few thrusts he delivered. He shuddered some. Eyes closed with lines between them that gave away the fact he was trying to concentrate through the feeling of being inside me.

"Uh-oh," I teased, squeezing my walls around his shaft on purpose. I wasn't able to pull them in much since Luke filled me to capacity, it seemed. "He's about to nut first. Like I predicted. What a shame."

He opened his eyes to mine and froze.

"It's okay, *LL*." I held back a menacing laugh. "I won't tell anyone you busted your nut on impact... or maybe I will."

He snorted a laugh. "I'm *not* about to nut. Your pussy is tighter than expected. I can admit that." Luke moved his arms from behind my thighs and astride me to in front of my thighs, using his forearms to hold them back, spreading me open for him more while angling himself against my spot. "But I'm good now. Had to get acclimated to your grip. 'Cause you're gripping me like you'll never let me go."

I moaned at the pressure this time.

"If there's one thing I am, suburban girl..." He resumed moving in, then out, but this time deeper, and angling up. "... is a man of my word. So I'mma stop playing with you."

His strokes thereafter were so deep I could feel him stimulating my cervix. My dance with pain and pleasure had me moaning more than I wanted to moan. He moved at a steady pace, never faltering, hardly switching it up. Just repeated applied pressure to one spot in one direction. Consistently. Never letting up for anything, not even his own exhaustion.

I couldn't help but moan louder. Couldn't help but to take it. I wouldn't dare to say it was too much at one point. I didn't have time to anyway because that pressure eventually morphed into something else.

Something powerful enough to have my walls spasming like a heartbeat and beyond my power. I tried to gain control over the fluttering by pulling my quivering walls in, but couldn't. After that, I was free-falling.

I locked eyes with Luke.

"Yeah, I feel that." He smirked. "I feel you feelin' it."

I fisted the sheets beneath me.

"Feels good, right?"

I couldn't respond, not with words, at least. Only sounds, noises, expressions that were foreign to me.

"Can't talk, huh?" He teased. "Hmm, Juliette?" He held his bottom lip with the bite of his top white row of teeth. Thrusting deeper with each word spoken.

I fought to keep my eyes on his, but I was feeling something stronger than me take over. It made my lids grow heavy. Made my eyes want to roll to the back of my head.

The sensation was so new to me. It was so intense and extremely *different* from what I'd ever felt before that a part of me worried a little. I don't know why worry was the feeling to emerge in that instance between Luke and me, but it was very much there. Present and making my heartbeats hammer so hard, I thought my heart was pulsing in my chest.

And I guess that materialized into a certain expression on my face. Because Luke took one look at me, and the cocky appearance he'd been drifting in and out of since we started gradually faded away.

He kept stroking though, much slower now, still going deep. The sensation he stirred in me by simply sliding in and out pulsated in tandem with my heart and grew stronger at the point of penetration, beneath those tacky ass sheets.

He squeezed his eyes closed and swallowed hard, his Adam's apple bobbing in his throat as he refocused on me.

Luke gazed down at me with a much softer expression. Softer than any look he gave me that night. Sincere eyes moved with mine like he was reading and recording things to memory.

I searched his eyes for something familiar, hopeful I'd find the answer to what the hell he was making me feel in my moment of uncertainty.

On cue, Luke instructed me to, "Ease into that good feeling with me, Juliette. Calm down, baby." He wet his lips slowly. "Just breathe with me."

His voice was soft, deep, tender. Comforting and protective now. It was all the things and *everything* I didn't even know I needed to hear until that moment. "I got you. You're good."

We held our stares.

"You're safe with me," he whispered.

I exhaled my anxiety and relaxed into the feeling, releasing all of my resistance to the tension that kept my muscles tight.

My eyes rolled closed. I pressed my head into the pillow, angling my chin up to the ceiling. Inside me throbbed successively with a sensitivity that consumed me completely, undulating back and forth like breaking waves on a coastline. The force was brand new to me. I couldn't figure out how to handle the pressure. So I did what felt natural. I gave into the urge to curl my toes and to arch my back. I braced myself for whatever came next. Hypersensitivity everywhere had me experiencing pleasure in my mouth as my tongue brushed the roof of my mouth.

Without thinking, my hands reached for his backside to hang onto something, *anything*, but I quickly pulled back, forcing my arms at my sides.

"You wanna touch me?" He asked in my ear. Luke took my wrist and guided my hand along his skin. "You can touch me. You can touch me wherever you want."

So I did.

Feeling as his gluteal muscles flexed repeatedly against my palms while he thrusted slower, deeper, and with so much consistent control. I couldn't help but to spread my thighs wider to accommodate more of him.

"*Good*, Juliette." He moaned between each word. "That's it, baby. Take me just like that."

My name said in his voice and uttered with so much passion,

only charged up the sensation rolling through me evermore. I had no choice but to submit to it.

So, I did.

Fearlessly.

Surrendering and breathing to the rhythm of Luke's breaths that had grown louder between us. I rocked back and forth beneath him, resisting nothing, leaving my limbs loose, trusting him to lead our dance. I inhaled when he inhaled and exhaled the same way, too, holding nothing back. Not even the sounds I'd never heard myself make until that night.

I had to fight exceptionally hard through what I was experiencing to whisper, "Keep... going."

"What you gon' do for me in return if I do that for you?" He whispered back, speeding up just a little. "*Hmm*? What you gonna do for me if I listen, Juliette?"

I moaned loud in defeat.

"Mmm," he groaned in response to my moan. "You gonna keep coming like this for me?" Luke thrusted slow and circled his hips in time to his breaths. "You gonna keep throbbing and coming on me like this, beautiful girl?"

I opened my eyes to him, gazing at me through the slits in his lids as he delved deeper. He pressed his hand to the side of my face and his thumb to my lips.

"I promise to keep going..." He bit his bottom lip and grunted. "... if you promise me, you'll keep coming. Aight?"

I fisted the sheets.

"Deal?"

I nodded quickly this time.

"Good." Luke used the pad of his thumb to pull my lips a part then lowered his mouth to mine to kiss me. His tongue stroked my tongue with the same speed and intention he stroked in and out of me with between my thighs.

And it completely opened me to him after that.

I moaned in his mouth, whimpered beneath him too. I totally accepted defeat while gracefully losing our bet.

* * *

The next morning, a touch to my shoulder woke me.

It was hard to open my eyes. The tired was still in them heavily. I attempted to lift my lids, but everything was too blurry to see.

My senses slowly returned when I felt cool air against my bare nipples.

"Juliette."

The coldness in his tone knocked the sleep right out of my eyes, allowing me to focus up to find him standing over me.

Luke had on the clothes he wore the day before. He had on his coat and sneakers, too.

Seeing him fully clothed made me aware I was naked and made me self-conscious. I grabbed the floral patterned comforter, pulling it up and over my breasts as I propped myself up.

Our eyes met, and he cleared his throat, breaking eye contact to glance at the door. "I got the call from the mechanic. He repaired my car and confirmed it's ready to pick up, so we can go."

Not exactly the first words I thought I'd hear from him, especially not after everything that happened the night before.

"Okay, *umm...*" I searched around us for a clock. "What time is it?"

"Time to go."

I focused up at him again to find him diverting his eyes once more.

My brows gathered over my eyes in response to his reaction.

"Get dressed," he ordered next, turning to head toward the door. "I'm gonna get my car and will meet you in the parking lot. Be quick."

And just like that, he left the room.

I remained in bed for another moment, genuinely confused.

Almost certain I imagined everything that happened the night before because...

"What the *hell* was that?"

That couldn't have been the same man who talked me through pleasure I'd never experienced before. The same man who couldn't keep his hands off me or his dick from inside me to the point we barely got any rest.

It surprised me to see he could get out of bed after all that.

And the *all that* I speak of wasn't only one round. It was three. The whole thing lasting for hours off and on.

I kicked the bedding off me and walked to the bathroom to freshen up, starting with a shower.

Questions and confusion cluttered my mind. We made so many poor decisions last night. Poor decisions I would consider making again, to be honest.

But only with him.

A quick soap up and a rinse was all I did before I was over the motel sink, ripping plastic off a pre-packaged complementary toothbrush, then drawing a line of toothpaste on the bristles.

I glanced up in the mirror and did a double take at my light brown skin. Above my collarbone on both sides of my neck were tiny red hickeys scattered here and there.

Just the sight of them brought with it a flood of flashbacks that made me shiver.

I hadn't imagined it. What I remembered Luke and me doing happened.

Then why was he acting so weird? Especially after what we showed each other?

I didn't take long in the bathroom. I brushed my teeth, rinsed my face with cool water, then pulled on my team-branded sweatsuit, slipping my feet in the sneakers I kept in my bag, and left the room wearing a hooded puffer coat and with my gym bag swinging from my shoulder.

As stated, Luke was waiting in the parking lot with his car parked facing the door of the motel room we stayed in.

The car looked just as good as how it looked when we left LU the night prior, and that pleased me to see the mechanic did a good job.

Luke's eyes met mine through the windshield before he moved them off me to focus on something else outside.

I brushed off that reaction. Ignored how distant he was when I got in the car, although he was sitting right next to me. For the first ten minutes of the ride, I waited for him to speak. Waited for him to break the silence with anything, even if it was an audible exhale. But nothing. I definitely wouldn't be the one to start the conversation. So by the time I saw the sign displaying the exit for Brookville University, I reasoned I would say something once we arrived outside of my school.

The lawns of the campus were empty, with students out and about doing their best to make it out of the cold.

Luke had stopped near the entrance to the parking lot when he put the car in park.

"Thank you," I started, unbuckling my seatbelt. "I really appreciate you doing this."

He nodded. "You're welcome."

Luke said that to his front windshield and not to my face or to my eyes. That made me jerk my head back.

"Luke, what's up?"

He released a deep breath.

"Last night happened and then today you're acting like *this*?" I gestured at him. "What's your deal?"

"You're back on campus," he answered, still avoiding eye contact with me. "I told you I'd drop you to your school, and that's what I did."

"You know damn well I'm not *talking* about that."

He licked his lips and rolled the back of his head against his headrest.

"I mean, you won't look at me, which is strange as fuck. Because last night—"

"Was last night," he said, shooting me a glare. "And today is today."

His usual sincere eyes were ice cold and empty.

That took me aback.

He laughed cynically. "What you want from me, shorty? A proposal? You want me to marry you now, or something? Like, for real, for real. What the fuck do you want?"

I squinted my eyes at him.

"Let's not make what happened between us about shit, aight?" He leaned away from me. "It was nothing. We fucked, we enjoyed ourselves, had a good time—"

"Fuck you, Luke," I threw back with more breath than tone.

I couldn't find my voice to say it with my chest.

Couldn't find it to save my life.

"Didn't I say we did that already?" He flashed a sleazy grin. "Quite a few times too, so trust me, baby. I remember."

My eyes pricked with tears and I had to ball my lips to keep them from trembling.

His eyes softened in reaction to my reaction for only a beat, though. Because a second later, he snatched his attention off me, entirely shutting his eyelids as he turned to sit forward in his seat.

I stared at his side profile for another moment before I reached in the backseat for my bag and left his car. Because if I stayed another moment sitting this close to him, I'd make the ten o'clock news that night for strangling his ass to death. I just knew it.

When I got out of his car, he said, "Juliette."

I paused, keeping my hand on the passenger door's visor, eyes honed in on his.

I thought this would be the moment he realized he was being a jerk and would apologize. Ask me to get back in the car so we could talk about what happened between us because I couldn't have been the only one who felt *something*. I couldn't have been the *only* one who felt the earth move the first time we had sex, or the second, or the third, time. Something *happened* between us. And I'd had enough sex to know it was definitely *more* than sex.

He ran his hand down his thick lips slowly, tugging on his goatee for a second before he said, "Make sure you stop by a pharmacy and get you one of those Plan B pills, 'cause I'm not interested in being anybody's baby daddy now or never. *Definitely* not yours."

My jaw dropped and I couldn't hide it. Couldn't help the urge of wanting to create not only a scene outside of my school but an entire blockbuster movie going ape shit crazy on Luke. Because I would. Oh, how I really wanted to lose my religion on his ass.

Rage brewed in my veins, boiling my blood, raising my pressure, and I knew I had to create space between us, and fast. So instead of saying anything in retort, I slammed his door closed really hard with all my might, watching the passenger window shatter before my eyes...

... like my heart.

"YOOO!" He shouted inside the car, turning away, hands flying to the top of his head. "What the fuck?!"

I stood there, silent, staring at him through the broken glass that had tiny, jagged holes where glass used to be near the center. A deep breath later, I stormed off, remorseless and angry at myself for letting Luke have the parts of me he had the night before. Because the guy I spent the night with was probably still in that motel room in Kaysville.

Sitting in the car I walked away from was the guy I vowed to maintain an unbreakable hate for, for the rest of my life.

I promised myself I wouldn't let that happen again, whatever happened in Kaysville. From that day forward, I vowed to never let a man get as close as Luke Lockett got to me.

I'd rather die one thousand deaths before I ever let a man get me like that again.

three

LUKE

"LUKE, you don't think you took things just a little too far?" My sister, Joy, asked in my ear. "Like? Not even a *little* too far?"

I stepped off the faculty elevator, moving my phone off one ear and on to another.

"Of course he *doesn't* think he took things too far," my other sister, Hope, echoed. "When does he ever acknowledge he's done too damn much?"

I kissed my teeth.

"Will you two shut up?" Faith, my third sister, the eldest, hollered on the line. "Just chastising the man. My goodness. Give it a rest already."

"Thank you," I finally expressed. "Damn."

"I am sure Luke had his reasons," Faith insisted.

I nodded my answer, not wanting to get into it. Not today, at least.

"Hi Coach Lockett," a student greeted as she and a group of girls passed me in the hall. She smiled and waved, and the rest of the girls giggled as she shushed them loudly.

I smiled but didn't reply.

"Well, if he has a reason for showing his ass at Saturday's game?" Hope challenged. "Why hasn't he told any of *us* about it?"

Because I had no interest in getting into any of it today. Not with their emotional asses, at least.

The *thing* that had my sisters all in my ear via a conference call the youngest of my sisters Joy conferenced was why I was on my way to the athletics director's office as we spoke.

A moment in time everyone thinks I wish I could take back, but if I could do it all again. I absolutely would.

"You didn't have to shove that old man like that, Luke?" Joy started up again. "Not in front of all those cameras. You have so much to lose and such a short fuse. What a terrible recipe for disaster."

I clenched a fist in response.

"And let's be very clear," Hope voiced again. "We have been defending you against all others who try to come for your neck over what happened at the game at Brookville. But between you and me? You were wrong, baby brother."

I sighed.

"Stop it," Faith defended. "We weren't there. We only know what the media has allowed us to see. You know how they *love* twisting stories and making *us* look bad on TV."

My big sister Faith would defend me to the end and on everything. Probably murder, even if I held the bloody knife in my hand. At my big age of 32-years-old, she still saw me as the baby brother in diapers she helped raise when she was a junior in high school.

But she was right this time. I *had* my reasons. I just didn't think I needed to say what they were.

"Happy Valentine's Day, Coach Lockett," another student crooned as she batted her lashes. I crossed the pedestrian bridge to the building my meeting would take place.

Like the young women before her, she smiled with all her teeth, eyes sparkling with something I wanted nothing to do with.

I smiled, then chuckled to myself.

"I see Langston U still got the hot in the asses girls we used to have to beat off you with a stick," Faith joked. "The players change, but the game remains the same, huh?"

Joy and Hope laughed, and I did too, grateful for the change in the subject.

"Oh!" Joy chimed in. "Y'all remember when we used to create a calendar of days we would pop up on campus without warning just to make sure Luke wasn't getting distracted by them?"

"Cockblocking asses," I mumbled, smiling. "I used to *hate* when y'all did that shit."

"Kept you out of trouble, though," Hope added. "Now didn't it?"

I'd arrived outside of the athletics director's office when I announced, "I got a meeting with the AD. I'll talk to y'all later?"

"The AD?" Hope asked. "Does this meeting have something to do with what happened at Brookville?"

"I don't know," I answered. "Maybe. Either way, I gotta go. I love y'all, but don't call me with this shit after today. You hear me?"

They all expressed discontent in their own way in response to my parting words.

"Yeah, yeah, yeah. Whine all y'all want," I decreed over them. "But I'm very serious."

"I'll call you tonight and you can tell me everything," Faith insisted. "It's okay."

"You better not call Faith and not me too," Joy added.

"We'll just conference a call," Hope suggested matter-of-factly. "Like right now."

"Hell no," I stated. "And I'm not calling anyone about what I discuss in *my* closed-door meeting. "Love y'all. Get off my phone. Goodbye."

I disconnected the call immediately after and turned my device off.

My sisters were my backbone. They loved hard and would go to war for me, but even they could grind my nerves with their overly protective antics.

The athletics director letting me know on my way out yesterday he had my assistant put a meeting block on my calendar didn't surprise me. Since the game the Saturday prior, I had heard nothing from him about it, although my assistant coach told him everything that had happened. But I knew the talk with me was coming.

"Luke," Brian, Langston University's Athletics Director, greeted me as I stepped into his office.

He wore a smile and a designer gray three-piece suit, and held out his hand, waiting for me to accept.

Brian Brady had been LU's AD for thirty-years and counting. He was the AD when I was a student and he never missed an opportunity to remind me. Tall like Kareem Abdul-Jabbar and with a voice and smile like actor Keith David, Brian had the warm and welcoming personality I needed right now.

I held his hand in a tight grip when close and he pulled me in for a hug and a pat to the back.

I was still getting used to my role as a coach at the school I attended once upon a time. Never did I imagine I would return to LU after leaving the country over a decade ago to play basketball in Spain.

"So," he started, rounding his desk to take a seat behind it. "How have you been?"

I inhaled a deep breath and relaxed in the armchair opposite him.

The game last Saturday was a tense one, long before it started. As one of the two last games against our rivals, Brookville University, before we played in the conference tournament, the energy was high and so was the drama.

"I'm annoyed," I answered. "To be honest."

Last Saturday's game had my team competing against Brookville's Lions - a team still under the coaching guidance of Coach Eddie Salvatore. Salvatore has been coaching for Brookville for years. Including the four years I played for Langston. He was an asshole way back then when I wore Langston's jersey, and judging by how shit went down between us the Saturday prior, age had not changed Salvatore one bit.

"I can imagine," Brian replied. "You know, your rise to the top at LU has pissed off many people."

"To be expected." I shrugged a shoulder. "Haters gone hate."

He chuckled. "I've always liked how you take things to the chin and not give two shits about it. It's something Walters always loved about you and why he wanted you back at LU."

After graduating from Langston in the spring of 2011, I moved to Madrid, Spain to play basketball internationally. I could've stayed in the states, play in the NBA, but I was desperate for a significant change and I figured living outside of the United States would satisfy that desperation. And it did... for a time. So, I decided at the start of my senior year at LU I would play overseas when I declared eligibility for the draft. I'd already traveled to Spain before graduation, to meet with the coach out there, with my agent, and believed I would play long enough overseas to retire out there. But then I couldn't shake my homesick feeling five years after moving to Europe. So I returned home to the states.

"When Walters told me you'd returned from Europe and was coaching a boys' basketball team at a high school in Brooklyn, he said he wanted you back here at Langston in the role of an assistant coach. I was all in," Brian began. "Walters and I used to grab drinks after work and he'd tell me all the time about you suggesting plays at practice when you were a shooting guard at the university. I thought that kind of leadership could continue to thrive here at LU. What a vision of success for one of our own players to return to the place that helped cultivate him after experiencing success outside of Langston U."

I leaned back in my seat.

I was only visiting LU to attend an exhibition game in 2019, show a little school spirit. In an arena full of people, Coach Walters recognized me the moment I walked in, inviting me to stand beside him on the sidelines for the entire game. I told him what I was up to, coaching high school basketball and he told me LU needed me more than any other school and he needed another assistant coach.

Brian balanced his elbows on his table. "Walters was always a visionary, so I didn't question his choice to bring you on board. And I'm glad I didn't. Because you've been an asset ever since."

A year after attending that LU game, Langston U hired me as an assistant coach for LU's men's basketball team at 29-years old. For two years, I worked alongside one of the greatest coaches in the history of men's basketball at Langston University. Last summer, all of that changed.

"Now I know Walters's passing took a toll on you," Brian acknowledged. "It did on all of us. His death was sudden. Here today, gone tomorrow. But you've risen to the occasion immaculately since day one."

Last summer, in late June, I got the call from Coach Walters's wife informing me that Coach Walters had died from a massive heart attack. I'd literally just spoken to him on the phone three days before. He was still red hot about losing to Duke University in the final sixteen during March Madness and vowed he'd get Langston another championship trophy the following year. It was three months after that losing game, but it still bothered him how close we were to winning the NCAA National championship. Coach Walters was a big guy with a big heart. Few people could say they didn't like him. We all felt the loss deeply, even with school on break for the summer.

Two weeks after Coach Walters's passing, I got a call from Brian and our university president requesting my presence for a meeting at LU. It was there they asked me to step into the role of head coach.

The first feeling felt was one that was overwhelming. Head coach at LU was never a role I considered assuming. But I wanted to pay it forward.

Coach Walters did more than just coach us. He mentored us, helped raised so many Langston U men. Took us on as his sons. My pops was very much a solid figure in my life, but my relationship with Coach Walters was different. The different I gravitated towards within minutes of meeting him when he watched me from the bleachers at the high school he scouted me at 17-years-old. I was a better man because of him. And I wanted to be that for the young men after me.

So I accepted my promotion, and they announced me LU's head coach for their Division 1 men's basketball team in August of last year.

And that's when the drama began.

"So with all that said," Brian concluded, "I want you to know I got your back."

I nodded.

"What happened last Saturday? What I heard Coach Salvatore said to you? Almost made me call that fucker up myself to give him a piece of my mind. None of what happened was your fault. I know everyone on that court at Brookville *knows* it, but they are doing a real good job of spinning shit in their favor, Luke."

With my promotion came a lot of envy outside of LU. Most university basketball team coaches who coached teams that played us on court were balding and graying old white men like Coach Eddie Salvatore at Brookville.

The moment I accepted my new role as head coach, I made history becoming the youngest head basketball coach at Langston University at 32-years-old.

I swaggered when I walked, wore my Langston U cap backwards and Jordans on my feet at school games where the press was present.

I had waves on a full head of hair that shined beneath the lights of every college arena we played whenever I removed my cap. I never tried to switch up who I was to fit in to the culture other coaches upheld. As a result, sports press was obsessed with the young black coach at Langston and the domino effect of that immense admiration was many people finding it difficult to see me be black, blessed, and brilliant.

"Bix College Hoops on The Sports Report keeps airing that fucking video from the other night," Brian complained.

"Brookville has right-wing sports media on speed dial and right-wing media always answers," I replied. "So what?"

"Our university president isn't happy with it, *that's* what, Luke."

I kissed my teeth.

"I know you don't give a fuck and to be honest with you, I don't want to give a fuck either, but the university relies on donor dollars to stay in the black, Luke," he explained. "Make no mistake about it. Langston U is a profitable business and our university president is the CEO of this profitable business. If he sees an area that may affect the university's profits, he's going to get worried. And when he gets worried, he requests people's resignation letters, if you catch what I'm throwing."

I clenched my jaw.

"Listen," Brian continued. "Donors hold the power to affect LU's profits. And, Luke, donors don't like—"

"Niggas?"

"Controversy," he corrected. "Negative press."

I shut my eyes and released the breath I inhaled.

"We received a call from the editor-in-chief at For The Culture. They want to do a story on you."

"Over this shit?" I quizzed. "Come on! It's just a little video of me shoving that dumb bigot out of my face."

"It's a *little* video that's matured overnight into a pain in the ass and has gotten close to one million views in seventy-two hours that most of sports media is trying to label as unhinged behavior. And they got the receipts," Brian reminded. "Let's not forget the number of arguments you used to get into on the courts when you played for LU, especially whenever we played Brookville."

"They're our rivals," I countered. "Things are supposed to get tense between us leading up to the conference championship."

"I scheduled the interview for tomorrow evening, Luke," Brian continued, despite my objections. "You'll sit with a Juliette Hart and will tell her everything. And I mean *everything*."

I stopped listening the moment I heard her name. My heart felt like it ceased beating, although I'm sure that was all in my head.

I straightened my back in my seat immediately. "Hold on, wait, back up a little." I leaned in. "*What's* the name?"

"For The Culture."

"No." I shook my head. "The journalist's name."

He peeked down at his notepad's paper in his hand and read, "Juliette Hart, why?"

My chest tightened this time. All I could do was blink repeatedly. A rush of memories flooded my consciousness, making me light-headed, my throat dry.

I had to force myself to pull it together.

Besides, it couldn't possibly be *her*.

"Nah, nothing," I answered low. "No reason. Just asking."

Brian stared at me for a beat, eyes analyzing the fuck out of me, which I didn't need. Not after hearing *that* name.

What were the chances?

"Hmph, okay, well," he continued, "I'll have my assistant send you the when and where of the interview—"

"Brian, I don't know about this one, man."

"Luke," Brian started. "This is a great opportunity to get your side of things out there. For The Culture has an excellent volume of readership, as pointed out in the phone call with the editor-in-chief. Many of the writers on staff are LU alumni, I've learned. I'm sure they've assigned a journalist who will tell your story from a different angle, a more auspicious angle. And let's be real here." He looked me right in the eyes. "You need *all* the help you can get, brother. You're doing the interview, Luke."

* * *

After concluding my meeting with Brian, I returned to my office to do a little research.

It was difficult for me to stay focused in the meeting with my AD after he mentioned the name of the woman who would interview me for the magazine For The Culture. Questions and concern bogged my mind, all centered on if the woman was who I thought she was.

So the moment I got back in my office, I parked myself in front of my computer at my L-shape wooden desk and immediately started googling the name Juliette Hart.

Before our night at a motel in Kaysville, I never knew the name of the girl I ran into in Brookville University's parking lot in the winter of 2008. Didn't even know she was on the cheer squad until the day after when I saw her on the sidelines with the rest of Brookville's all-girls cheer squad, shaking their crimson red pompoms during our first rival game that basketball season. There was something about her I was so drawn to. She was curvier than the other girls. Thick thighs, round hips, and a soft waistline. Just perfect and with a face highlighted in tiny brown freckles that was equally distracting. She had hair I rarely saw on black girls. Juliette was a natural red head with frizzy bouncy curls that reflected a deep copper hue underneath arena lights. The volume of her hair and how it framed her face resembled a lion's mane. She had the most beautiful baby doll eyes. But my fascination never stopped there. Because her lips were what I'd become a little obsessed with staring at, at every game against my rivals. God shaped her lips like a heart. Then did the same with her face. And interestingly, the shape of her waist and her ass resembled an upside-down heart, too. While her waist was small, her stomach wasn't flat at all and that intrigued me the most since all the girls at Brookville seemed stick thin, but

Juliette didn't care to be like the other girls. She was thick with a confidence that was even more attractive than her outer appearance.

Her picture was an easy find online during my initial search. She indeed *did* work for For The Culture. Had been working there since 2018, according to her online portfolio. She was an investigative journalist with articles published in their magazine and their online blog. On the blog I found her headshot, and her photo was what I'd been staring at for close to half an hour. Big, beautiful copper curls. Face still shaped like a heart, a little fuller, and sexier. Lips so plump they almost appeared animated. As if an artist had drawn them on her face with a very steady hand.

I sighed in thought about those lips, remembering how they felt against mine.

I only learned her name after she was in my car and on the way to her school. A name just as beautiful as the girl herself. A name that every time I whispered it the night we spent together, it made my dick hard... which is why I loved saying her name so often.

"Aren't you the new campus crush?" I heard at my front door.

I clicked the x at the top of my computer screen, closing the web page window, collapsing the zoomed in picture of Juliette. I lifted my gaze to find my colleague Delilah leaning on my doorjamb.

She smiled and walked her leggy frame closer to my desk.

"There were some girls outside the office gushing over the video of you practically squaring up with Brookville's coach on their court last Saturday."

"Good girls always like the bad boys at some point in their lives." I leaned back in my seat. "It's a phase. They'll get past it."

"I don't know." She licked her lips while taking a seat in the chair opposite my desk. "*This* good girl hasn't seemed to grow out of that phase just yet."

Okay, so Delilah was *more* than a colleague. She and I had been seeing each other off campus after our hookup following a faculty Christmas party two years ago. I'd just left dinner with my sisters a day earlier, which was more like an intervention-like discussion about why I hadn't settled down yet.

The same sisters who every chance they got during my college years, consistently reminded me never to trust "these girls" because they were all starving for a come-up and my sisters were not about to let their *come-up* be me.

They had cause to be concerned.

There were some incidents at LU. Girls in and out of the university, poking holes in sealed condoms before sex with popular players when the players weren't paying attention.

Everyone knew Langston U as a basketball school. The school infamously handed out scholarships to underprivileged young black men, often from the hood, specifically to help Langston University to win conference championships and National Championship Games every year. And our Division 1 conference *loved* watching Langston advance in March Madness, because the more rounds we advanced to and played in the NCAA tournament, the more units our conference received. Units represented money from the basketball fund - the pot of money earned from allowing a major television network to air the NCAA Division 1 men's basketball tournament. That pot of money gets distributed to the Division 1 conferences for every round a team from that conference played in the tournament, except for the championship round. And each unit is worth over a quarter million dollars for each round, each team makes it to. The goal was always the National Championship Game for the university, though conferences don't earn units for championship games. But if we made it to at least the Final Four round, our conference could really cash in.

So best believe, everyone financially affiliated with LU had investments and were happy to benefit off of a Langston U men's basketball player.

And if Langston's basketball players played their cards right, our young black men often got a degree out of the deal because of their full-ride scholarships. More than often, they got drafted into the NBA.

Some of the most talented basketball players, past and present in the league, were alumni of LU. If you played ball at Langston, everyone almost expected you to declare eligibility for the NBA draft before graduation. So an LU men's basketball player had a target on his back before he played his very first NCAA game as a freshman every November.

Despite that, I always felt my sisters were overly protective of me to a fault and their fear of me getting into trouble in college with girls on campus became my fear. Then, in adulthood, their fear of me being alone for the rest of my life became my fear too... a fear I've used way too often to make decisions.

Not excluding deciding to date Delilah... if we can even call it *dating*.

"Got any Valentine's Day plans?" She asked.

Delilah worked in LU's bursar's office and we met my first day as assistant coach at LU. She never made her attraction to me a secret and had tried many times to get me alone. But there was no genuine spark between us. Just sex. A lot of intercourse that hadn't been happening as often as of late.

See, I only entertained her advances because I didn't want to be alone for another winter, years after my permanent return to New York City. My sisters are all married, have husbands, and families of their owns. So their lives had shifted, and I was starving for a shift, too.

So Delilah was someone *to do*. She didn't start that way. I tried to see something more in her, but the connection was far too superficial. So she went back to being just someone *to do* to me. And she only became that when I realized I was using every chance with her to get to know her and she wasn't doing the same with me. Instead, she was using every chance she got to let the world know we were together. Whether it's a photo of our dinner plates and her tagging me on social media. Or an over-the-top birthday post that included my picture and practically a love letter in a caption form, showboating our romance that wasn't a romance at all.

And I've ignored it, letting it slide, until recently, when I learned she was doing the same thing with someone else.

"Working," I answered, clicking the button to put my computer on sleep mode. "The Valentine's Day plans I got are romancing these plays for Saturday's game."

She pouted her pink painted lips. "That sounds no fun." Delilah moved to the edge of her seat. "We should hang out. Do dinner or something."

"I think I'm gonna spend today alone."

She stared at me for a moment with her tongue pushed into her cheek. Delilah released a nervous laugh, then asked, "Luke, are we cool?"

"I don't see why we wouldn't be."

"Ever since you saw me out to lunch with Cal last month, you've been distant."

Cal, short for Calib, was the assistant professor of biology, who had a large social following online. His short but informative science videos often went viral on social media because he recorded all of those videos shirtless.

And to be clear, I hadn't just *seen* her with Cal *at* lunch.

"I just figured," I started, "since y'all spent New Year's Eve and New Year's Day at a lodge in the Poconos together, things had gotten serious between you two."

She got quiet.

"I mean, based on the picture y'all took together and that you posted in your social stories."

"Oh, I... *um*... hmph. I didn't..." Delilah cleared her throat and scratched the back of her head. "I didn't know you saw that."

"Because you didn't tag me in that one?"

She scoffed a laugh.

"Delilah, it's cool," I told her with a smile. "We're cool."

"I guess I should've asked if you had a problem with me seeing someone else."

"I don't."

I did.

"We were never exclusive," I added.

But I also don't like to share and I shouldn't have to tell you that.

I wasn't seeing anyone else, so I figured she wasn't either. That was my mistake, I guess.

"So you're good, Delilah."

"Am I though?" She was at the edge of her chair. "I mean, what was I supposed to think? You've never been open with me. Never expressed a relationship was something you were interested in. I can never get a good read on you to see where I stand in *whatever* it is we got going on here. The only thing that has ever been crystal clear between us is sex, so..."

"Hey Coach," one of my basketball players greeted, as he walked past my opened office door on his way to the basketball court.

I shot a glare at Delilah. "What's good, Villard?"

Delilah has used every opportunity to let the world know we were together. But giving insight into my business to outsiders, especially my players, has never been my thing.

"Look, I'm not trying to get into any of this here since obviously it isn't the time or the place," I started. I'm happy for you, Delilah. And I think you should see where things go with Cal."

'Cause I sure as hell know we're not going anywhere besides back and forth on this. And I'm done doing that too.

"And you're right," I told her. "I haven't been a simple person to read and I apologize about that. But the truth is, I haven't seen that for us in some time now and I should've been clear on my feelings and not just clear about sex."

She blinked a few times in response.

"I do have to get back to work though, so..."

"Yeah, right," she stated dryly and with a forced smile. "I'll go. Take care, Luke."

If it were possible to say *fuck you* politely, Delilah's *take care, Luke* would qualify as the alternative.

I watched her leave my office, then refocused on my computer screen, waking my computer up with a tap on the trackpad.

Eager to get back at it, I reloaded the web page I closed out to reexamine Juliette's headshot for a few more moments. I focused in on her eyes, wanting to know everything behind them.

Was she happy?

Single?

Did she think of that night as much as I did?

I always knew of her before that night in the motel, but I never knew her personally. But what we did in the small town of Kaysville, New York, stuck with me like an exhilarating experience I couldn't shake or quit wanting to relive. Powerful enough to bring me - a guy who believed he mastered keeping his guard up with the opposite sex - down to his fucking knees. That night eventually pivoted my perspective on what I thought I knew about intimacy... and what I craved from it, forever.

THEN... THE KAYSVILLE MOTEL, KAYSVILLE, NEW YORK – SUNDAY, FEBRUARY 13, 2011...

LUKE

MY LIDS FELT one hundred pounds heavier than the night before. I was *so* tired, I unintentionally ignored the ringing at first. I blinked my eyes opened when I couldn't continue to sleep through the chiming, quickly realizing it was my cellphone ringing with a phone call.

The device was on the side table on my right. At least it *was* my right last night. This morning the side table was behind me and not because it moved.

I moved.

I found my arms draped over Juliette's soft waist when I blinked my eyes opened. She laid asleep in front of me, completely unmoved by the ringing phone that had finally stopped.

I lifted my head off the pillow, then slowly removed my arm from off her waist. Then I realized we were both naked. And soon the events of last night started returning to memory gradually, like the sunlight attempting to fade in through the motel room's cheap sheer curtains.

The ringing started again.

With no opportunity to process what I was recollecting and with my phone ringing again, I turned to the side table behind me and snatched up the device.

An unfamiliar phone number flashed on the screen, but I answered anyway.

"Hello?" I answered, more suspicious than groggily.

"Morning, son," a gruffly old voice said in my ear. "This is Griffen, the mechanic who's working on your car this morning? We met last night when I towed your Honda to my auto shop."

"Right, yeah," I acknowledged, feeling foolish for sounding on edge when I answered. "What's up?"

"Your car's ready when you are," he confirmed. "I changed your axel and your flat tire. The shop is less than fifty steps from your motel room door. I'll be here when you two are ready."

The indirect mention of Juliette had me shooting a glance her way.

She was still asleep. The bedding contoured against her curvy form. I had to blink back the lusty thoughts watching her elicited and the rush of blood hardening my dick.

"Uh, yeah, thanks." I rolled off my back and up to a seated position. "I'll be there in about ten minutes."

"Take your time," he told me before I ended the phone call.

I lingered in a seat for a few minutes at the other end of the large bed, trying to get my head together. Last night was far from anything I was expecting, far from what I planned to do.

I ran my palm down my face, doing my best to gather myself and my thoughts. My morning drowsiness had the effect of a hangover. Like I had a lot to drink and partied hard when liquor never touched my lips last night.

I staggered to my feet and headed to the bathroom when I glanced Juliette's way, doing a double take. She looked so beautiful asleep. Mouth slightly opened as she inhaled even breaths while in slumber and let them go the same way. A smile tugged at my lips and then quickly fell when I spotted the condom wrapper on the carpeted floor.

A condom wrapper that froze me in place and immediately sent me into a silent panic.

I'd gotten up an hour after we finished having sex.

Soon after Juliette and I came, we went to sleep, too tired to do anything else. I'd left the bed to discard the condom we used in the toilet before returning to bed and finding Juliette already asleep. And the moment my head touched the pillow again, I drifted right to sleep too.

Knowledge of what we'd done the moment my eyes opened to a dim room in the middle of the night had me staring up at the popcorn ceiling, willing myself to go back to sleep an hour later.

Instant replays in my mind of what we'd done had me so rock hard, my dick tented the bedding I covered with. I always kept a condom in my wallet at the insistence of my father. While the women in the house made me promise to leave the girls at school alone and to focus on my studies, my pops was more realistic. Besides asking me about my grades and basketball practice, he'd often ask if I had a condom in my wallet.

It came in handy tonight and I was grateful for it. But now I wanted more of Juliette but had no more protection.

I tried palming my hard-on, hoping the pressure would help it go down, but I couldn't seem to get my urge, my new craving for this girl, under control.

I rolled onto my side and moved in close behind her. Pressed my nose to the back of her neck and inhaled her while sliding my arm around her waist.

Everything in me said, turn back over and go to sleep. I'd experienced the girl I'd been daydreaming about ever since running into her in her school parking lot. Seeing her was the only highlight in playing Brookville U every year besides beating them.

And what she and I did was good. It was great. We had fun while it lasted, and it was time to be responsible again. But her skin felt so warm and soft against mine and I didn't want to fight wanting her... or the opportunity to experience her again.

Just one more time.

"Juliette," I whispered against her neck.

She inhaled a deep breath and released it slowly.

I brushed my lips against the back of her neck. The decadent scent of her body lotion drew me closer.

"Juliette," I repeated against her, needing her to hear me. I needed her consent more than I needed her. And I needed her badly.

She stirred in front of me before stretching her arm behind herself to hold me at the back of my head. That made me nuzzle my nose more against her honey brown skin. Made me want to be inside her even more desperately.

"Yeah?" she asked softly.

"You down for more?" I asked. "Can we..." I took a breath to hide how badly I wanted her. "Can we do it again?"

She nodded first and whispered, "Okay."

I balanced myself on an elbow to lift my back high enough to look her in the eyes. She turned onto her back to focus up at me.

"I have no more condoms."

And saying that shit out loud should've brought me back to reality. Like a whiff of smelling salts to restore my common sense.

But it didn't.

And I hoped it didn't for her either.

"Are you cool with that, Juliette?"

She nodded her answer again, then asked me, "Are you?"

A tall three-headed lamp post light outside of the motel room door lent light to the room, making it dim with a sepia tint. So I could see Juliette's eyes searching mine for something after I told her that.

Maybe for me to change my mind?

I had no intention of doing that.

"Yeah." I swallowed hard, clenching my jaw. "I'm cool with it if you're cool with it."

She only allowed a few seconds more to pass between us before she agreed again with, "Okay."

I barely knew this girl. Had only learned her name hours prior, and I only asked for her name because I thought it would be odd to drive in a car for two hours with a stranger.

But now here I was, getting in position to penetrate her raw, and I wasn't giving it a second thought.

We inhaled together when I slid in from behind, feeling wet warmth devour me from the head of my dick to the shaft.

I shuddered a little at how hot and how softly she molded around my dick. Shuddered so hard I had to close my eyes tight to gain some control over myself.

I experienced everything sooner than I did with a condom. Every grip and twitch of her walls, quiver of her slick inner folds. I felt when her pussy got wetter from the friction I created sliding in and out from behind as I spooned her.

Her moans made composure impossible to have with all the new stimulants happening between us.

Before that night, having sex unprotected had been a devilish thought to play with but forbidden to do.

Between my sisters and my mother warning me about "them fast ass girls" and Coach Walters's several speeches about the repercussions of men thinking with their dicks and never the brain God gave them, I knew better. The men in my life trained me to reject the idea of fucking raw.

But... I don't know what happened.

Something about this girl named Juliette had me willing to risk everything, including my sanity.

I stood over the sink, splashing cold water on my face, reminded in that moment I didn't pull out when I came.

Pressed my palms on either side of the vanity and dropped my head to my chest, letting it hang there for a moment.

Last night seemed so unreal. Even while in the act, everything felt like a mirage. A wet dream, but in real life.

That's the only reason it did not alarm me when warm hands skated down my chest two hours after I came inside Juliette. I didn't give it another thought.

She wrapped her fingers around the girth of my dick and started jerking me off slowly. Her hands switched places with her mouth when I moaned, alerting her I was up... and on the brink of nearly losing my mind.

It was still dark outside, so I knew a new day hadn't broken, and I couldn't believe we were up again.

My view was a little blurred from fatigue, but I could make out Juliette's face and her mouth on me. Her lids were low as she bobbed on and off me. Frizzy copper tendrils from her high bun framed her beautiful face as she slid me in and out between her lips.

"Juliette," I groaned, pressing my head into my pillow to calm down. The sight and the wet sensation of her giving me head were too much to witness at the same time. Had my hand gripping her curls to compose myself. I believed I'd burst if I didn't.

She looked so tired, eyes red rimmed, but she was probably feeling what I was feeling a couple of hours ago - an insatiable need pulling her out of sleep.

So I answered.

"Come here," I whispered as I used her hair to slide myself free from her mouth. Didn't want to come like that, anyway. I wanted to make this time last.

Plus, I didn't want to cheat myself from indulging in my new favorite view...

Watching her come undone.

I guided Juliette closer to me by her biceps and took her by the waist, assisting her to get in position to straddle me. She balanced herself on her knees, held me firm in her hands and slowly lowered her hot pussy down on my hard dick.

Her head slung back. She gyrated her hips back and forth, pressing a hand against my chest for leverage as she worked us up to a rhythm between us that was all breaths and a squeaky box spring beneath our mattress. I balanced myself on my elbows, wanting to catch her every expression. She was intoxicating in action. I was drunk off whatever this was between us. Clearly out of my mind and committed to insanity because this right here, the connection we had in this seedy ass room felt so pure.

It felt too fucking right to be wrong.

I dropped my head back between my shoulders, allowing myself to get lost in the motions. I fit so perfectly inside her. It was like the very existence of her walls was only for me to occupy the space between them.

Juliette and I locked eyes when I leveled my head. Her breasts bounced with her movements, light brown skin glistened with sweat from only riding me.

Her eyelids fluttered, brown nipples pebbled before my eyes.

And I got greedy, not wanting for this to end so soon.

"Control it, Juliette. Please," I pleaded, pressing a hand to her lower back to slow things down. "Don't you come yet. I'm begging you not to fucking come yet."

"I can't..." she shook her head slowly from side to side. "I can't control it and I don't want to."

She whimpered, dropping her head back between her shoulders, as her walls contracted and released around me.

"Come on," I gritted, frustrated. "You gotta control it with me."

"I don't know how," she whined.

I sat up and changed positions, lying her on her back, and never disconnecting.

Her moans grew louder as I delivered deep strokes with literal reckless abandon in my attempt to catch-up to her. She mumbled things I couldn't make out, but she sounded so sexy, whining and moaning in between her words.

"Mmm-hmm," I whispered against her neck while sucking on her skin. "Talk sweet to me, just like that."

My dick grew harder, my pulse raced. Heat consumed me so much, I couldn't figure out if I was in the heat or if the heat was around me. I also couldn't resist coming any longer.

I dug my fingers into her hips and the soft feel of her skin against my trimmed nails sent me over the edge. My strokes became staggered, breathing ragged. Her eyes did that thing I liked. That thing that drove me buck wild and made my dick harder than it already was.

In reaction, I thrusted harder, faster, deeper, watching her like a movie as her perfect mouth fell open and the only thing visible in her eyes were the whites in them.

"Gahdamn, Juliette," I panted. "Ahhh, fuck!"

My arms quaked on either side of hers as I shook the bed beneath us, fighting like hell to keep myself upright.

The mattress shaking caused friction between the box spring and the bed's frame, amplifying my concise strokes. My mouth formed a trembling O when heat morphed into a coil in my gut and finally a rush of pure raw bliss that seemed to radiate throughout my entire body. A heightened sense of awareness seized my mind, and I didn't want to disrupt it. Everything sounded and felt so fucking good around me. Juliette's wet pussy, her sounds of pleasure, the slap of our sweaty bodies colliding, and the loud squeaks from the bed's old ass box spring. Everything had me in a state of sensory overload. I'd felt nothing so phenomenal. Never experienced that amount of pleasure in my life. I wanted to get lost in the rush more than I wanted to breathe. Just as quickly, my body took over and acted on instinct. I pumped in and out of her involuntarily, damn near chasing my nut like a feign. My eyes were closed when I felt her soft hands caress my lower back before she laid her palms flat against my glutes to hold on. I opened my eyes to hers and refused to blink. I wasn't only greedy for her touch. I was greedy for every expression she made while I was deep inside her.

Juliette was very expressive with me. She showed every feeling she felt on her face and it was such a turn-on for me.

Silent moans turned into guttural grunts and groans from the both of us, powerful enough and with more than enough volume to bounce off the ceiling and walls. We created the sexiest duet of moans and pants in time *to my last thrusts until we got too carried away with coming to make even the slightest sound. Both of our mouths hung open in slacked jaws as we shared a lustful gaze, neither one of us looking away. The bed's squeaks and our slick bodies colliding beneath the bedding grew louder in our arrested silent stare. The muscles at the base of my dick contracted like crazy in response to her walls quivering around the shaft. And I refused to pull out, refused to take my eyes off her. Because then I'd have to break eye contact and leave the comfort of her velvet walls, ruining the beautiful flow we created.*

I couldn't have that.

I trusted Juliette, even though I didn't know her. And I was so enthralled, so transfixed by the feeling between us and her staring back at me while coming, I allowed myself to let go too.

I tunneled even deeper, coming inside her with stuttered strokes. And doing that left me drained and exhausted. I had nothing left to give, so I gave into gravity, collapsing on top of her.

After I brushed my teeth with one complimentary toothbrush and cleansed my skin with a quick shower in the motel shower stall, I stood over Juliette, fully dressed. I watched her as she slept, observing the natural rise and fall of her chest.

So fucking beautiful.

Ethereal.

I was so regretful but also so enamored. I'd never experienced such a mixed bag of emotions at one time in my life. Not after getting into my first choice college with a full-ride scholarship, not after shooting the winning shot during my first game as a freshman. The feeling I got with Juliette the night before was something that scared the living shit out of me. Scared me because I wanted to do it so many more times again and, in the same way, changing nothing. Which was dangerous as fuck.

I cleared my throat and said, "Juliette."

She gave no response.

I moved closer and laid a hand against her soft shoulder. "Juliette."

I stepped back when she stirred this time; the covers slipping off her breasts because of her movements. My eyes went there. I was getting erect in my jeans, staring at her nipples again.

Her eyes finally opened, and she looked up to find me standing over her.

She grabbed the comforter next, pulling the bedding up and over her breasts as she sat up in bed.

Our eyes met and my heart did something the moment our eyes locked, something I didn't need it to do right now.

I cleared my throat, breaking eye contact with her. Just us looking at each other was making me weak for her again.

"I got the call from the mechanic," I told her. "He repaired my car and confirmed it's ready to pick up, so we can go."

"Okay, umm..." Juliette checked around herself. "What time is it?"

"Time to go," I answered.

She refocused on me and I snatched my eyes off her again.

Her hair was in a disheveled top bun, lips slightly crimson from our destructive behavior the night before. But what really made me uneasy, but still turned-on, were the very red hickeys I tattooed all over her neck with my mouth.

"Get dressed," I told her next, turning to head toward the door. "I'm gonna get my car and will meet you in the parking lot. Be quick."

I exited the room right after.

* * *

I said nothing during our sixteen-minute drive to Brookville U. I was too busy replaying in my mind last night's events. From my peripheral, I saw when she kept checking to her left at me. Likely searching for eye contact so we could talk.

I *really* didn't want to talk.

I couldn't help but to feel embarrassed. Shorty probably thought

I did shit like this all the time. That's what I would think if I were Juliette.

I didn't know how to explain that I didn't know what got into me last night and how stuff like that didn't happen often to me.

Didn't happen at all, actually.

I'd never had a girlfriend and I could count the amount of partners I've had on one hand... including her.

The women in my family made me promise not to touch those girls on campus because they were nothing but trouble. But I was still a man. A man who had pussy thrown at him daily just for getting out of bed. That promise to keep my dick in my pants at all times had all the makings to be broken. I stayed true to fucking none of them raw, though. I wasn't ready to be a father. Damn sure not ready to catch anything worse than pregnancy.

But then Juliette happened and changed all that in one night.

She wanted to talk. I could feel it in her frustrated sighs ten minutes into the car ride. The tapping of her nails as we neared the exit for her school. Even as I pulled up outside the gate to her school, feet from the parking lot's entrance.

Brookville University had the most beautiful campus I'd ever seen. A campus constructed specifically for collegiate brochures. The few polished students making their ways around campus resembled the youth models photographed on the billboards in Manhattan.

Especially the one sitting next to me in my car. No one would've known she'd spent the night in a cheap ass motel just looking at her.

I wanted to give her more than that because she deserved it. But I didn't have it, nor did I have the time to get it just to give it to this girl I barely knew. And since I couldn't and I couldn't make sense of the shit that went down between us the night prior, I decided it would be best to be done with her... for her own good.

"Thank you," she said, unbuckling her seatbelt. "I really appreciate you doing this."

I nodded because it was all I could do. "You're welcome."

Couldn't make eye contact with her either. Because if I did, I would've caved to the desire of wanting her to stay. This need to continue to enjoy her company.

I decided I had to fight it.

She was from a school whose university culture I hated.

Pompous, classist, uppity, downright unwelcoming.

Juliette had been none of those things in the time we spent with each other, didn't exude that energy at all, but she was friends with people who were. And since I barely knew her, she couldn't be exempt from that... right?

She *had* to be the same as them.

Why else would she choose to go to school here?

"Luke, what's up?"

I released the breath I didn't realize I was holding.

"Last night happened and then today you're acting like *this*?" she deduced next. "What's your deal?"

"You're back on campus," I answered, eyes focused on the lush green lawn of her campus. How it was so green in the middle of winter annoyed me. "I told you I'd drop you to your school, and that's what I did."

"You know damn well I'm not *talking* about that."

I licked my lips and dropped my head against my headrest, rolling the back of my head left and right. She wanted answers, and she wasn't wrong about wanting them. I just couldn't give them because I didn't know the answers yet myself.

I was so unsure. I had never heard of or seen anything like what happened between us, happen between two complete strangers. She made me question those deep feelings and why I had any for a girl I didn't know.

The people in my circle never encouraged me to feel what I was feeling for her back then. I never thought to search for it either. So when those feelings found me and because of Juliette, I did not know what they were or what to do with them.

So, I did what I knew how to do.

Reject the unknown.

"I mean, you won't even look at me, which is strange as fuck," she continued. "Because last night—"

"Was last night," I spat.

She wanted me to remember. I could see it in her eyes. She wanted me to remember that thing that I felt, that I'm sure she felt too. But I couldn't. It was too scary, too much of a mystery to me, and made me too weak in the knees.

"And today is today, shorty."

I forced myself out of feeling sentimental.

Laughed cynically to downplay my feelings, praying it would help me get through this with her. I needed her out of my car and out of my life.

"What you want from me?" I quizzed. "A proposal? You want me to marry you now, or something? Like, for real, for real. What the fuck do you want?"

She narrowed her eyes.

"Let's not make what happened between us about shit, aight?" I shrugged. "It was nothing. We fucked, we enjoyed ourselves—"

"Fuck you, Luke," she whispered.

"Didn't I say we did that already?" I forced a grin. "Quite a few times too, so trust me, baby. I remember."

The hurt in her eyes made my chest ache. They were cloudy with tears and her perfectly shaped mouth was gradually morphing into a pout. That bugged me. God, that bothered me so much. I was the reason for her sad reaction. Made me want to reach for her, apologize, and surrender to the unknown. But...

... I couldn't.

This was never supposed to happen. At least in my immature mind, it wasn't. I felt weak around her and that scared me. And instead of addressing the feeling with honesty and a need to be understood, I shutdown, not wanting to give Juliette that kind of power over me.

Because I barely knew Juliette, but I wanted to lasso the world, to give to her, just to see her smile.

And the fact that I would go to great lengths just for her approval made me extremely uncomfortable.

I snatched my attention off her, shutting my eyes closed as I turned to sit forward in my seat. I hoped she'd take a hint and leave so I wouldn't feel compelled to have to explain myself.

She reached into the backseat for her gym bag, opened the door, and stepped out of the car.

"Juliette."

The same uncontrollable feeling that led me to wake this girl from sleep to have sex unprotected was the same uncontrolled feeling that made me call her name when she finally got out of my car, like I wanted.

I was so conflicted.

So confused by those feelings.

So interested in what if.

What if she went to Langston and not Brookville?

What if she made it on that bus and I didn't have to volunteer to drive her?

What if we just went to sleep last night and kept our hands to ourselves?

Would I still feel the way I felt for her that day?

She paused closing the door to lock eyes on me.

I ran my hand from my lips to my goatee, unable to come up with an answer to any of those questions. So my punk ass told her, "Make sure you stop by a pharmacy and get you one of those Plan B pills, 'cause I'm not interested in being anybody's baby daddy now or never. *Definitely* not yours."

It wasn't the kindest thing to say, probably the worst thing to say in that moment, but I meant every word. I didn't want to be only a baby daddy. I wanted to be a husband and a father, like my pops and Coach Walters.

And I didn't want a baby daddy kind of relationship with Juliette.

But she took my words at face value. The reaction on her face of shock and anger was the proof. Instead of saying something back, she slammed my car door closed so hard, the passenger window shattered. Shards of glass shot at me and I had to put my hands up and turn away to stay safe.

"You're safe with me."

I gave her my word, and I meant it at that moment. But the water in her eyes as she stared at me through the cracks of shattered glass was enough proof I'd fucked up.

But even with that, her doing that to my ride pissed me off.

"YOOO!" I shouted inside the car, pressing my hands to the top of my head. "What the fuck?!"

She didn't speak another word to me, didn't shout or try to kick the rest of the glass in. Juliette turned and walked off and I did not know that moment would be the last time I saw her.

* * *

"You've been having some kinda luck with this car here this weekend, huh?" Griffen, the mechanic who repaired my Honda the first time, expressed with a chuckle.

He'd just screwed in the last screw on the passenger door. Griffen needed to remove the door panel to install the new glass window on the passenger side of my car. The door panel was back on and that's what he was working on, securing in place.

I passed through Kaysville again to see if he could take care of it. It was along the way back to Manhattan, and Griffen's prices were reasonable. I damn sure didn't have it like that back then, surviving off a weekly allowance from my parents. Money, I liked to save more than spend. I prayed like hell as I drove down the interstate from Brookville to Kaysville that his shop handled window replacements. Because if I had to get my parents and sisters involved, needing to tell them how the glass got broken to begin with, what an actual nightmare that would've been.

Feeling the cold air push through the holes in the shattered glass on my way to Kaysville was a sobering feeling and a reminder of why I wasn't ready for no fucking girlfriends.

"You can't wash your car or roll this window down for the next 48 hours," he explained. "You keep your car in a garage?"

"Nah," I answered. "In my school's parking lot."

"Hmph," he huffed, dusting debris off his hands. "Well, that should be fine too, I guess."

His shop was small, with car parts here and there. For an auto shop, it was spotless, with smells of rubber and metal competing for dominance in the air.

"You're tall," he commented. "You go to the fancy school close to here? That Brookville? You play basketball over there?"

"No. I'm a student at Langston U in Manhattan. I play basketball there."

He smiled an all-white smile. "A city boy."

That got a little laugh out of me, which was much needed.

"Your girlfriend goes to Brookville, then?"

I sucked my teeth loudly. "How many times I gotta tell you she ain't my girlfriend, man?"

He glanced at me with the same raised salt and pepper brow he gave me the night before on the side of the interstate.

"Mr. Griffen, sir."

"Much better."

I chuckled.

He approached his black steel mechanic's cart, which wasn't far to pick up a roll of blue tape. "You two remind me of me and my wife, Abby, when we were younger."

I sighed, wishing he'd hurry so I could get back on the road and to Manhattan, and put this entire weekend behind me. I did not want to hear about his damn wife, Abby.

"Before we were married," he started, stretching the tape from the top of the newly installed glass on the passenger side of my car. "Many, many years ago, she used to date my next-door neighbor, Samson. So I'd see her almost every day after I returned from high school before they broke up that summer. I'd say hi whenever we crossed paths because it was the respectful thing to do. A sentiment she didn't share because she never said hi back. Never made it a mystery she didn't like me, either. And I couldn't understand why because I was a pretty likable guy."

I laughed.

"I wasn't sure if it was my face or something I said." He chuckled. "It couldn't have been what I said, I reasoned, because we barely spoke more than one word to each other. Me always doing most of the talking, anyway."

He smiled at me.

"About a year later, my senior year in high school, me and a few of my friends visited a local diner here in Kaysville, only five minutes from this shop. Well, two minutes after we arrived, the same pretty girl with a smile and shape like Pam Grier—"

"Pam Grier?" I interrupted, smirking. "Let me find out the missus was bad."

"Oh, she was bad, son," he confirmed. "Whew, was she bad? Sure as hell was! Still is if you ask me, but let me get to the good part of the story."

I relaxed in the metal chair and smiled, waiting.

"So we're sitting at the table and Abby walks over wearing her server uniform. Turns out she's our server for the evening. Abby addresses everyone at the table, all except for me."

"Damn."

"I know!" He hollered a laugh. "That's what I said. Literally. Damn."

I laughed into my fist.

"She asks for everyone's order, all nice and sweetly. Gets to me and asks me all nasty, 'what do you want to eat?' And if I'm being honest, she didn't ask that in the nasty I would've liked if you know what *I* mean."

"Yo!"

He laughed out loud. "I got my food, ate it, and enjoyed my time with my guys, but I tasked myself with understanding why this girl, who I barely knew, hated me so much."

"So then, what happened?"

"Oh, will you look at that," Griffen teased. "*Now* the city boy's interested in this old man's tale."

I snorted. "Yeah, aight."

He snickered. "What happened was, I left her tip on the table, a big one, and bid my guys farewell outside of the diner, then opted to wait in my car for her to end her shift. I had this vintage yellow Ford Mustang my parents gave me for my 18th birthday and as an early graduation gift since my high school graduation was in three months. I did not know when her shift would end, but I resolved myself to waiting in my Mustang for however long I'd have to wait because I just had to know what Abby's problem was with me."

I nodded my understanding, hanging on to every word. The way Griffen told a story made it impossible not to be invested.

He had finished with my window minutes ago, but I hadn't moved an inch. He was right. I was very interested in how his story ended.

"So three hours later." Griffen took a seat on his work stool and spun to face me. "She finally steps out of the diner, in her uniform, but now with a purse on her arm." He pointed at me. "I wouldn't dare do this now, but back then, the 80s? People weren't uneasy about people sitting in their cars and approaching them in parking lots. At least Abby wasn't."

"I got you."

"I announced myself, of course, and she and I make eyes from across the lot. She stopped walking and waited for me to approach and I had this long drawn out speech that I decided against giving and spoke from the heart."

"What you say?"

"I told her *'Abby, I'm Griffen, and I don't know if you remember me, but I live next door to your ex-boyfriend Samson. From the time I saw you walking out of his house and until tonight, I've realized that you have a grudge against me and I have never understood why.'* Abby folded her arms and said nothing in response, so I continued by apologizing."

"Wait." I pointed. "*You* apologized to *her*?"

"I did. I said, *'I want to apologize if I ever said anything to you that would make you not like me because, although that is unlike me to say anything hurtful, I must have done so for you to hate me so much.'*"

"Smooth." I bobbed my head up and down. "I see what you did there."

He smirked. "I then said my only question to her was, *'what did I say to you so I know not to say it to someone else?'*"

"Okay."

"She batted her long pretty eyelashes and half smiled at me and told me, *'it wasn't what you said, it's what you've done, Griffen,'* in the sweetest of voices. So, I asked her what did I do?" He smiled to himself. "She told me, *'what you've done is to be so devilishly handsome to me it's become distracting, and that infuriates me, Griffen. Because frankly, I don't like you having such a hold on me.'* Boy, I had the laugh of all laughs that night."

I smiled with all my teeth.

"That woman hated me because she liked me." He laughed so hard his shoulders shook. "How backwards is that?"

"Crazy," I answered through my laugh.

"And I was crazy about her. Asked her to marry me the summer after my high school graduation. We've been married for almost 40 years with five children, all older than you." He grinned. "And two grandchildren with another on the way."

"Dope."

"Some of us don't know how to express our feelings. Many of us don't even know what they mean when we feel them. We don't show ourselves grace by sitting with those feelings long enough to make sense of them with a purpose to question or understand them. And as a result, the rest of us are misreading each other and jumping to conclusions about issues we could've easily sorted out and mutually understood by simply talking."

I twisted my lips to one side, knowing exactly what he meant.

"You were very protective of the girl you came here with last night," he explained. "You two seemed very familiar with each other, like y'all had been together for a while." He grinned. "It was a pleasure to be around and nice to see young spirited love—"

"Love?!" I snorted. "Please. She's a stranger. I barely know that girl."

"Didn't seem that way to me." Griffen chuckled. "Not even a little. There was a comfortableness between you two. Like I said, you two seemed like you've known each other for years. That was the first thing I noticed when I pulled up beside you in my tow truck at the side of the interstate. That's why I thought she was your girlfriend."

"It was an interstate," I reasoned. "I offered to drive her back on campus because her school team left her behind at my school after our game against them. I was only making sure she got back in one piece, is all."

"You cared," he acknowledged. "So much so, you went out of your way for her. Why would you do that for a stranger?"

"She had no other way to get back on campus. I was only keeping my word, man." I clenched my jaw. "I think maybe you're looking too much into the situation."

"Or maybe," he countered, standing to his feet to run a dry cloth over the newly installed passenger side glass window of my car. "Just maybe I saw something between the two of you that you haven't seen yet yourself because you're too busy getting in your own way." He laughed knowingly, while gesturing at my car. "You're all set to go."

I drove back to Manhattan with a lot on my mind. Filled with a lot of what Griffen said, a lot of what happened at Brookville with Juliette, and even more of what happened the night prior at the motel.

I went back and forth with my feelings about it all, seeing where I was wrong, regretting some things while wanting to fix others.

By the time I returned to Langston University's campus, I decided at the upcoming game at Brookville the following month, I would pull Juliette to the side, apologize, and see what that yielded.

But that game came and went, and she wasn't there. I searched for her copper hair in the crowd and amongst her cheer squad so many times, looking for her left me distracted throughout the entire game. So distracted, I got the ball stolen and missed a few shots. We lost the game that night, but losing didn't bum me out more than knowing I might have lost an opportunity with a girl I may have had genuine feelings for. The reality I would never see Juliette again was something I had to force myself not to care about a week later. Because the conference tournament was shortly after and graduation from LU would come next, and I wasn't about to fuck any of that up over being distracted by some girl. I had no time to get caught up on any girl, actually. And my sisters were sure to remind me of that when they saw me slipping those weeks after the night at the motel.

In my free time before graduating, I'd look Juliette up online after learning her full name.

Juliette Hart.

Such a beautiful name for a beautiful person.

And her name and the girl herself would be a source of my fantasies for several years after.

LUKE

I ENTERED through my front door and walked into silence. The faint scent of my cologne mixed with the bergamot incense I burned the night before were the only things there to greet me.

A view of Manhattan at night and the Hudson River in the distance, courtesy of my floor-to-ceiling windows straight ahead, calmed and recharged me immediately. When I made New York home again almost six years ago, I was undecided on what borough I would choose to live. But I knew wherever it was, it would offer a view of the water. I learned overseas how rewarding the view was, waking to the sounds and views of water in the distance.

My kitchen light was the first to get switched on since it was closest to my front door. I swaggered to the floor lamp in my living room next, switching it on before relaxing on my L-shaped sofa.

A rolled cigar laid in the ashtray on my glass and wood coffee table waiting to be cut and lit. Beside it was a silver butane lighter and the matching cigar cutter.

The day's events, which included the meeting with my AD, the conversation with Delilah, and two meetings afterwards - one with my team and the other with my assistant coach - were all pushed to the back of my mind. I felt like I was moving around my day like a zombie after receiving the news about being interviewed by Juliette.

Like, really?

What were the odds of *that* shit?

I wondered if she was stressing over seeing me again, like I was about seeing her. Did she even remember me?

I mean, I'm sure she remembered me. I made sure of that. In college, one of my motivations behind going so hard on the hardwood whenever Langston played Brookville University at BU was specifically so Juliette would remember me after every game.

What I was curious about was if she thought of the night we shared before the moment she was told I would be the subject of her interview.

My phone chiming in my pocket pulled me from my thoughts. And I was thankful for the interruption.

A glance at my device screen brought a smirk to my face.

"What's happening, Trey?"

"Same things different day. How 'bout you?" Trey quizzed on the other end of my phone.

Trey and I have been friends since we were freshmen at Langston U. He used to ball for the school but now owned a Caribbean-African fusion restaurant in Hoboken, New Jersey with his lovely fiancée, Serenity.

"As good as I'm gonna be," I told him, reaching forward for the rolled cigar and the silver cigar cutter I always kept nearby. "What's going on with you?"

"I'm waiting for Serenity to finish with her makeup so we could head out for dinner, and wanted to call you to check in."

I snickered, turning the cigar side ways to clip the head. "So pretty much you're about to be waiting all night. How romantic."

"Shut up," he said, which made me laugh.

Trey was the last of my four close friends to bow out of the single brotherhood. And I knew he'd be next when he introduced the crew to his lady a few months after they started dating. Like I said, Serenity was a lovely woman, but I knew there was something more to Trey's obsession with Serenity other than her looks. He was in love. Getting older taught me that.

It was good to see him like that. And I was happy for him, but I never missed an opportunity to poke fun at the new man he'd matured into.

"I'm waiting for my woman so I can take her out for a Valentine's Day dinner in which after I'm coming home to go to bed, and I ain't going to bed alone nor am I going to sleep... if I did my job right," he boasted in response. "*You* are home alone. Just *you* and your cigars. Lonely as fuck. Like always."

"Gahdamn, Trey! Shots fired, fuck." I returned the cutter to my glass table, laughing. "See, why are you choosing violence on a loving day?"

He chuckled.

"I said one thing to you. One damn thing, and you over there comin' in hot."

Trey laughed some more. "How have you been, man? Like for real, for real? That video of you wildin' out at BU finally made its way down my timeline on one of my socials earlier today."

I squeezed my eyes closed, cringing a little, shaking my head. "Once it makes it on social media, it's all downhill after that." I placed the phone on speaker, then laid the device down on my coffee table in front of me.

"Nah, not this time," Trey insisted. "You weren't wrong and word on the street is, everyone else agrees. You had every right to go off like that, Luke. You were defending yourself. I hear there's an old video of Coach Salvatore talking just as reckless to his players."

"Yeah, well." I placed the cigar in my mouth to wet the area around the end I cut. "That video of his reckless mouth never went viral, so it might as well not exist." I shook my head. "The media has spun it so well, Brian is telling me he's set up an interview with a magazine so I can tell my side of the story."

"Good," Trey said. "That's great. Which magazine?"

"For The Culture."

"Nice," he said, excited. "FTC is a great publication. Serenity's a loyal subscriber. They publish more than enough decent content. That's a good look, Luke."

I held the cigar at a side angle and flicked the butane lighter on, rotating the flame around the foot of the cigar, toasting it. "Yeah, but here's where it gets real trippy."

"What's up?"

"You remember the girl I told you about senior year? The shorty I drove back to Brookville after her team bus left without her?"

"The one who fucked up your car?" He asked.

I sucked my teeth. "She didn't fuck up my car."

"Luke, she stuck your Good Samaritan ass with two car repair bills after you did her a solid offering to drive her back to BU."

I lifted the cigar to my lips to ignite. Puffing in and out, rotating the foot of the cigar around the butane flame a few times while filling my cheeks with bitter, spicy, earthy smoke. I moaned to myself as I released the fulfilling taste just as quick. "To keep it real with you? Her actions weren't completely unprovoked."

"Well, that's breaking news to me," Trey replied. "Because the way you told it, shorty was an unhinged menace."

I blew cigar smoke above my head, then peeked down at my cigar, nodding. Pleased.

A habit.

"Well, what about her, anyway?" Trey inquired. "The suspense is killing me."

I snorted. "She's the one who's doing the interview."

"No."

"Yes."

"Wow."

"Yup."

"How you feel about that?" He asked this time.

I held the cigar against the webbing of my index and middle fingers, wrapping my thumb around the tip. "I'm not sure."

"Hmph."

I took another draw from my cigar and blew out the smoke, squinting through the white smoke. "I didn't tell you every-thing that happened the night we got stuck in Kaysville together."

"Aight..."

"She and I had sex in that motel room." I licked my lips slowly. "*All* night long. Barely slept."

There was silence for two beats before Trey told me to, "Shut the fuck up."

I bust out laughing.

"Luke, say you're lying."

"Hand to God."

"*Wow*," Trey drug the word out. "That was unlike you. Hooking up with a stranger and keeping it to yourself—"

"She wasn't a *complete* stranger, though," I clued in. "Remember that night, freshman year, when we drove out to Brookville in two Suburbans with three other players, along with Sean and Siobhan from Langston's co-ed cheer squad?"

"Yeah." He answered. "To pull off the rival prank."

"Aight, so, you remember the girl I collided into in their parking lot?"

"Vaguely..."

"That was the *same girl* I drove out to Brookville years later. The same girl, now woman, I'm interviewing with tomorrow."

He was quiet for a moment, before saying, "Say word."

"Word."

"Whoa."

"I know, right?" I acknowledged. I placed my cigar in the ashtray and leaned back in my seat on my sofa. "Very wild shit."

"It's crazy how y'all paths keep crossing."

"Ain't it?"

"And always in a February."

"*Hmm.*" I took a minute to consider. "Shit. I don't know why I didn't notice that for myself. "

"I don't know, man," he started. "Shorty might be Mrs. Luke Lockett in waiting."

"Easy, man." I told him. "Easy."

"I mean." He laughed in response. "She must've been the exception for you to have kept you two hooking up in that motel to yourself all this time."

She was the exception.

"I don't tell you *everything,* Trey."

"Yeah fool, but back then you fucked and told." He insisted. "What made that situation any different? If anything, you would've got more brownie points for smashing a rival and telling everybody and their mamas. Now, *that* would've trumped any rival prank Brookville U could've thought up."

"Anyway." I leaned forward for my lit cigar again, needing a shift in our conversation. "Serenity ain't ready yet? Damn. What is she doing? Cloning herself over there?"

Trey cracked up laughing. "Luke, shut up."

It was silent between us for a few beats.

"You gonna tell her she's special to you at the interview?"

I wanted to deny Trey's claim that Juliette was special, but Trey was a true, good friend, someone who knew me through and through. Made no sense to lie or hide the fact she was special to me.

I sucked my teeth. "Man, why the hell would I do that?" I peeked down at my cigar before bringing it to my lips to puff. "I didn't end things on a friendly note, feel me? You remember how I was back then with them girls. My cut off game was swift and cold. To keep it all the way real with you, Trey? It surprised me she agreed to interview me, giving how we left things."

"Hmph."

Smoke slowly wafted out of my mouth. "Some things you can't take back."

"And some apologies are better shown than told," Trey preached.

"True," I concurred. "True."

PART TWO

2nd half...

"Love is a game that two can play and both win..." – Eva Gabor

six

BLYSS RESTAURANT, BAR &
LOUNGE, NEW YORK, NEW YORK –
TUESDAY, FEBRUARY 14, 2023

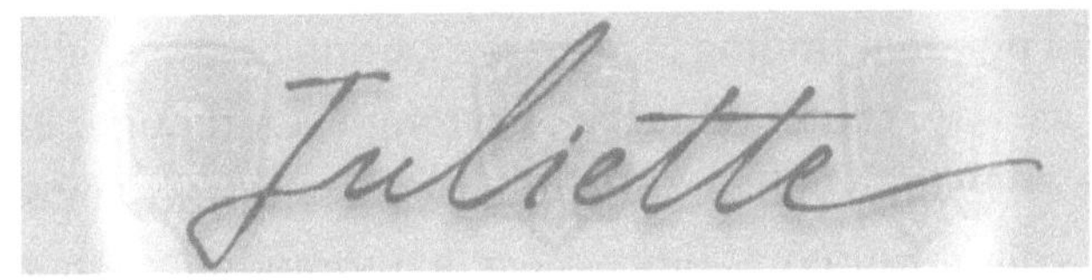

JULIETTE

"CAN someone tell me something ratchet already, please!" Clarke expressed with a sigh. "Them lawyers have kept me cooped up in their office all day conducting legal research, and I need something nonpolitically correct to help me escape."

I held back a laugh to sip my wine.

"I am *tired* of talking about work tonight," Clarke complained some more. "Give me something juicy to sink my teeth into."

Myself and two of my old college roommates, Clarke and Esme, lounged at a window seat at Blyss, a restaurant in midtown Manhattan. As predicted, couples packed the building on Valentine's night.

"Girl," Esme started. "I'm responsible for thirty kids, five days a week in an elementary school with no teaching assistant. That's the most ratchet you're gonna get from me."

I sputtered a laugh over my glass.

It was a good thing Clarke thought ahead to reserve our table from last week. We all were so busy with work, our usual Galentine's Day plans had to get pushed to Valentine's Day. None of us three had anyone waiting for us at home, so it was nothing for us to keep our commitment to meet up.

We'd all ordered red sauce pasta dishes on arrival and two bottles of dark burgundy wine to wash our food down. We were on our second glass individually, which meant it was a good time to tell them the news.

"So," I said. "I guess it's up to me to be tonight's entertainment, huh?"

"Don't disappoint," Clarke teased.

"Oh, girl." I smirked. "Never."

I could put on a smiling face for our outing because I didn't want my girls to suspect something was wrong even though, inside, my thoughts were like a bull on steroids charging through Times Square.

"My editor hinted I can expect a promotion to her role by Christmas."

Esme's face lit up and Clarke squealed.

I held a hand up to calm them both down. "Nothing is final yet, so let's not get all hyped and excited so soon, cheer team."

They giggled.

Clarke and Esme were well aware of my editor-in-chief goals and how hard I'd been working to get promoted.

"Especially when you hear what I have to do to get my name on a gold plaque desk sign."

"Ooh! That sounds sleazy, with a possibility of ratchet," Clarke commented. "Let's see where this goes. Go on."

I rolled my eyes playfully.

"Yes," Esme concurred. "Out with it."

"They want for me to interview Luke Lockett."

"Really?!" They dragged out at the same time.

"Yup." I inhaled a deep breath. "It'll be a cover story. Getting his side of things from the incident that happened at BU last Saturday."

"Isn't that like a conflict of interest or something?" Esme questioned. "You know, since *you* were a student at BU?"

"And hated him dearly," Clarke added.

"I didn't *hate* him. And even if I did, it wouldn't be a conflict of interest," I clarified. "It's an unfortunate coincidence and *unfortunately*, that's not convincing enough to get my EIC to reassign Luke's interview to someone else."

"If you didn't hate the guy, why on earth would you ask for someone else to interview him?" Clarke challenged. "This story is tremendous! No one is *not* interested in furthering this conversation. Why the hell would you think about passing this up? This has career making potential all over it."

As a paralegal who, to me, was overqualified for her job but kept failing the bar to practice law in NYC, my girl Clarke knew all the right questions to ask. And always.

I shut my eyes and shook my head.

"Don't tell me you're still upholding the BU versus LU rivalry." Esme fingered her tapered cut coils. "Even *I* put that beef behind me and to rest the moment I crossed the stage for my degree. And you know I used to go so hard for BU!" She laughed at herself.

I puffed my cheeks full of air and released it slowly as I gathered the courage to say, "Okay, listen. I am only going to tell y'all this once."

They both stared at me.

"I'm only going to tell the story *once*, because after that, that's it." I proffered. "You'll have questions. I already know you'll have questions, and I'll answer some of them, but not all because maybe talking about some of it will relieve the stress of it all."

"Well, spit it out already!" Clarke shouted. "With a warning like that, this better be good, Juliette."

Esme and I laughed at Clarke's reaction.

"Do y'all remember our last game at LU? The one I opted to stay behind in the city after to hang with my cousin Billie?"

"I remember," Clarke acknowledged.

"What about it?" Esme pushed.

"Billie never showed up that night and by the time I ran out to see if our team bus was still outside, y'all were all gone. Even the bus carrying the basketball players."

Esme perked up in her seat. "What?"

"Wait, wait, wait." Clarke's brows wrinkled. "Then *how* did you get back? Because you returned to campus on Sunday. A lot earlier than planned, but you came back like you said you would."

"Luke drove me back to campus."

There was silence at our table, so I told them everything.

I told them how Luke found me outside of the school without a ride home and with a dead phone. I told them about the dead deer, the flat tire and bent axel. Our motel stay and eventually about the sex.

"Juliette, wait a fucking minute!" Clarke hollered. "Because I *know* your red-headed ass didn't have sex with Luke *fine ass* Lockett and kept that shit to yourself for all these years. No, you did not!"

"Not the Luke Lockett with the crazy sisters who acted like his damn bodyguards," Esme added. "Because I've heard the stories of his sisters busting up in his dorm room to remove a girl or two by their hair."

"Okay!" Clarke broke up laughing. "Talk about it. Because that LU juice would make it *all* the way to Brookville, so you know it was news."

"I can't believe you kept this to yourself all this time," Esme whined.

The rim of my glass hid my smile. "I don't kiss and tell."

"Oh, my God!" Esme pressed her hands to either side of her cheeks. "So what happened the next day? Why did nothing come of that night?"

"Because he was a heartless jerk, and I should've known better." I released the breath I'd been holding. "He didn't want to talk about what happened. The sixteen-minute car ride was so awkward with us saying nothing. We finally get on BU's campus and the jackass's parting words to me is for me to get a morning-after pill because he's not interested in being anyone's baby daddy."

Clarke gasped. "You're lying."

"Sure wish it."

"I always knew he was an ass." Esme shook her head. "He was always so damn arrogant whenever LU played BU. Arguing and getting in players' faces. Real hood, honestly. Like? Why would he say that to you if you two used protection?!"

I tucked my lips into my mouth to rub them together.

"Because you used protection, *right,* Juliette?" Esme pushed.

I shifted my eyes off her. "The first time, yes."

"The first time, yes?" Clarke chimed in. "What the *hell* do you mean by that?"

I tapped my pink gel nails on our table's surface and said, "We had sex three times that night, *but...* he only had one condom."

Their jaws dropped at the same time.

"Okay." I held a hand up. "Was it wise? No."

"It was fucking stupid!" Clarke hollered. She checked around herself before refocusing on me. "Let's call that shit exactly what it was."

"Yes, it was dumb, but honestly, it was *Luke Lockett,* and... don't y'all judge me but... he flattered my young ass wanting to do that with *me.* I was a little curious about how it would feel too... having sex without something between us." I lifted, then dropped my shoulders. "My parents put me on birth control the summer before I moved to Brookville's campus, so I knew I wouldn't get pregnant. But yes, you're right. It *was* stupid. *But...* also, it was the *only* dumb risky thing I did in college, so it was whatever."

"So, like, okay," Esme jumped back in. "It happened, and clearly you didn't end up pregnant or worse, caught something awful."

"I got the pill as he advised, even though I was on birth control, just for good measure, because I *really* wanted nothing tying me to the likes of Luke Lockett for the rest of my life." I laughed cynically. "And I got an STD test done on campus the following week. So yeah, nothing happened after."

"I remember you being so closed off around that time." Clarke waved a finger at me. "That's why you refused to cheer the game against LU the next month. The one before the conference tournaments started."

"Yup."

"Oh my God, Juliette." Clarke frowned. "I wish you would've told me. You already know we would've driven out to Manhattan to key that motherfucker's car up!"

Esme and I laughed.

"Blasting Jazmine Sullivan's 'Bust Your Windows' on repeat and would've turned the volume all the way up when we arrived to do God's work," Clarke added. "'Cause, what?! Nobody would've done my girl like that and gotten away with it."

"And that's why I kept it to myself, because I didn't want the drama," I admitted through my laughs. I bit inside my cheek when I revealed, "I didn't want him to know he hurt me or that I was thinking about him after I got out of his car. He was finished with me, and I didn't want him to think the feeling wasn't mutual."

"Hmph," Clarke huffed.

"Because although how things ended between Luke and I was terrible, I thought I did something wrong at that motel."

"Something wrong, like having sex with him without a condom?" Esme asked.

"No." I bit inside my cheek, a little uncomfortable with what I would reveal next. "Something *wrong* like weird him out. Make things awkward."

They stared back at me, confused.

I closed my eyes and sighed. "My parents forbade dating most of my teenage years and only allowed it for my prom night. But by then I was so anxious and awkward around guys. And that awkward, nervous energy stayed with me when I moved on campus at BU my freshman year. The story was always the same. Guys liking me, me liking them but me not knowing how to talk to them, clamming up and getting shy around them until they lost patience and interest." I laughed at myself. "I didn't lose my virginity until sophomore year at BU and it was to my tutor. The only reason we got to do that was because I was failing chemistry and had to spend every day with the guy. So I was more comfortable with him than anyone else and could ask him if he would be so kind as to pop my cherry. My goodness." I covered my face, embarrassed, recalling that time. "And because I *had no* real discussions about sex with anyone or about what I'm supposed to feel when having sex, by the time I started having it, I was hoping to feel what the women in porn and in the movies felt. I kept trying to have the sex that would have me screaming and moaning and being all, whatever it is they are in porn and movies."

Clarke and Esme giggled at me.

"And when I wasn't feeling any of what I learned from porn and the movies, I started faking it because I reasoned that's what they were doing, and this whole shit about sex feeling so damn good was false advertising. I decided sex was just some over-hyped bullshit... until that night in Kaysville."

I licked my lips slowly, staring out into the restaurant. "The sex I had with Luke was nothing I *ever* experienced before in my life. To this day." I shut my eyes. "The feelings he worked up in me. The level and heights of pleasure I reached with him?" I blew air out of my mouth. "That was the night I learned firsthand that when you come? Like when you are having an intense, full body orgasm in real life? Your ass ain't saying shit!"

They laughed out loud.

"You literally *can't*." I giggled. "You're barely moaning, much less hollering. And when you are making a sound, you're not focused on it being sexy. I'll tell you that. You literally can't say or do shit because you're stuck in this state, in this trance. Voluntarily restrained in an invisible hold where the wave of sensations ground you in the *right now,* but you can barely remember to breathe because you're being stimulated all over and you just feel you're drowning in air. Your ears pop, then ring like crazy from the pressure building in you until all you can hear is your heart beating. Then everything ceases in you and around you and all you can focus on is coming and hoping the feeling will last forever, wondering where it will drop you off next." I closed my eyes and took a breath. "And trust me… you'll want to go wherever it goes because you become so bewitched, so mesmerized by the pleasure that you're positive you're going wherever the hell that pleasure takes you next, even if it's off a damn cliff."

My girls were so honed in on me, I wanted to laugh at how attentive they were being.

"At least that's what I experienced." I half shrugged. "I'd never felt what I felt with Luke and I couldn't hide it that night. Couldn't control it worth a damn. Eyes rolling, unable to keep my mouth closed. I was in complete shock at the rush I consistently received from having an orgasm. Saying indiscernible shit that didn't even make sense to me." I smoothed my hand down my copper curls. "I was making noises like an animal who lived in the wild, y'all."

Clarke snorted, and I burst into laughter.

"I was *so* fucking embarrassed by the morning." I laughed some more. "And he didn't want to talk about it. So, I didn't know how to approach the conversation. I wasn't sure if he felt what I felt because I *swear* I would've done *anything* Luke asked me to if he vowed to make me feel what he made me feel again, but for the rest of my life." I cackled. "But he didn't want to talk. Then he lashed out at me. Said the nastiest thing a guy has ever told me. I just figured…" I bit at the skin on my bottom lip. "… I weirded him out. Dude probably couldn't get me out of his car fast enough."

"Juliette," Esme said low, taking my hand.

I closed my fingers around her hand and smiled.

"I'm good." I assured. "After a few days of crying in the shower and sulking around campus, I moved on. I skipped the next game against LU, buckled down on my studies and made my books my bae and eventually work took its place and I married my career."

I twisted my lips from side to side.

"I'd be lying if I claimed I haven't been chasing the *spell* Luke had me under in that motel room, though." My eyes met Clarke's and Esme's. "That motel was the seediest, creepiest room I'd ever seen in real life, but somehow it was like paradise and that bed the real fantasy island come to life with us on it together." I shivered at the thought.

"Whew, God," Clarke looked up over her head to address the restaurant's ceiling. "I've seen what you've done for others."

"Clarke, please!" I chuckled. "Baby, you don't want these issues. Stop it."

Esme's humor wrinkled the sides of her mouth.

"Besides," I continued. "I don't want a man who will make me feel like *that* on a bed, but like shit off it." I picked up my glass of wine and leaned back in my seat. "I want a love I've always imagined having. I want a man to crave me, and to cater to my peace and I cater to his. Then and only then can *we* duplicate that rush of coming, make it everlasting and not just limit it to sex. I know it is possible in everything with the man I'm meant to be with."

My girls giggled.

"I want to feel passion on and off a mattress. Be open and vulnerable with a man who wants to be open and vulnerable with me. I want to feel safe. I want to feel love beyond words, you know?"

"Yes, girl," they expressed as a duet, making us all laugh.

"One day." I shrugged. "But today, we drink." I held my glass up for them to clink with mine, which they obliged.

Esme asked, "So, to be clear, you're ready for this interview tomorrow, right?"

"I have no choice but to be," I answered. "Because I have a lot riding on this interview, being the best thing I've ever written at FTC. And if it doesn't go well, I'll feel like everything I've done at FTC would've been a waste. I want that promotion once my editor-in-chief resigns."

Clarke and Esme bobbed their heads up, then down.

"What happened between Luke and I was years ago. He probably doesn't think of that night anymore." This time, I gulp my wine. "I'm confident Luke is mature enough for us to get it done. All I need is an hour, maybe two, in his presence to get what I need to write this article. That's it. It'll be easy."

At least, I hoped it would be.

seven

JULIETTE

I COULDN'T GET my hands to stop shaking.

Easy listening music played from the hotel restaurant. I tried to shake the tension from my trembling hands as I drew closer to the hostess stationed at the front of the restaurant's door.

"Good evening," she greeted me with a genuine smile. "Welcome to Mon Ami. Do you have a reservation?"

I hadn't spoken to Luke before tonight. Mykal and Luke's athletics director planned for Luke's interview. So this would be the first time Luke and I would interact on any level after all these years.

All I needed to do was to show up and do my job.

Hopefully, conducting the interview would be as easy as it seemed in my head.

I glanced inside of the restaurant to survey the scene. For a Wednesday evening, Mon Ami had quite a few patrons.

Surveying the scene turned out to be a mistake

Because out of all the people in attendance I could have focused on, my eyes slammed right into Luke Lockett.

And why was he staring back at me?

It was hard to put the moment we locked stares into words. I felt this pull between us when he pinned me with his gaze. One so powerful, I couldn't break free of it to look away.

The pull would have to be that magnetic, right?

Because what else could explain how, in a crowded room with me not in it yet, would we be able to find each other?

I forced the nervous energy, threatening to make me fall apart, out through my lips. Nervous energy conjured up from only us locking eyes.

He sat there, cool, calm, and relaxed. Definitely not as jittery as me. Luke's gaze was unwavering. Even as he lifted his glass of water to his mouth to sip.

"Yes," I told the hostess, forcing my eyes off him and redirecting them to hers. "My party is already here. The reservation should be under Juliette Hart."

A quick glance down at her clipboard, a smile and a gesture for me to enter, and I was heading towards him, closing the distance between us that had been there for over a decade.

I imagined this scenario many times after graduating from BU.

When our schools competed against each other, I always knew I'd see Luke next time. There was always a *next time*, because there was always another game.

But after graduation, our *next times* were up.

I came to terms with never seeing him again.

Why would we see one another *again*?

We didn't share mutual friends outside of school. We didn't even go to the same school.

But...

There would be instances when I'd imagine, sometimes in mind-movies that lasted for hours, what it would be like if we saw each other again.

What would we say to one another?

How would I feel seeing him again after all this time, given how we left things?

Unfinished.

Under dim lighting in a high-rise hotel restaurant with glints of light from neighboring skyscrapers and in a setting Feng shui'ed for romance was *definitely* not in any of my visions.

When I arrived at his table, I put my briefcase on the white tablecloth to remove my Burberry wool cape. I searched my closet for hours, obsessing over what to wear. I settled on a wool camel blazer, a black crop top with matching leggings, and knee-high leather boots. I covered all that with a wool hooded cape to brave the New York City cold.

I was comfortable and felt beautiful when I left my co-op in Brooklyn, but on the island of Manhattan and in front of Luke, I second guessed all that.

After he graduated, I kept up with his career moves. He signed with a team in Madrid, Spain and played basketball all over Europe. Doing well for his self overseas, helping his team to win a championship twice in the five years he played with them.

There weren't any interviews that documented him explaining his reason for ending his basketball career overseas to return to the states to coach basketball. I hoped he'd explain that part in his interview with me, more so for my curiosity.

"What's up, Luke?" I greeted, draping my wool cape over the back of my chair.

He bowed his head slightly. "What's good, Juliette?

Our first words to each other and it was uneventful.

He looked as good in person as he did on sports networks standing at the sidelines as LU's cool ass head coach. Still lean, with squared shoulders and a muscular neck. Skin still the clear dark chocolate brown of his youth. And he still looked young, like he would forever be in his 20s. His mustache goatee had matured into a full, sexy, coarse beard. Luke was still every bit of the heartthrob he was as a college basketball phenom. The allure was still very much there.

I plopped into my seat across from him and moved my eyes to my briefcase, unzipping it to push my hand inside in search of my notepad and voice recorder.

"This interview shouldn't take more than an hour, maybe two, at most." My hands were shaking again. His cologne mixed with something else emanating from him smelled so good.

Dammit.

Luke wore a burgundy pullover hoodie and distressed jeans, which I glimpsed beneath the table as I made my way over. Two simple things he wore so well. The hoodie's burgundy color contrasted beautifully with his dark skin.

I was delaying the inevitable, making eye contact with Luke again.

"So, straight to business, huh?" He asked in the deep raspy voice that made my heart plummet into my stomach. "No catching up, ice breaker, just straight to the point?"

I rolled my eyes over at him, not only frustrated at what he asked, but frustrated at the realization he would not make this as easy as I hoped.

"Absolutely," I said, shooting him a glare. "How else should it be?"

Our eyes met, and he licked his lips slowly.

I leaned forward in my seat to place the recorder at the middle of the table, doing my best to inhale even breaths. Lowered my eyes to my notepad to flip open and to find a blank page. "My questions tonight will range from what happened at BU, your tenure as head coach at LU—"

He grunted, causing me to stop mid sentence.

"This is already sounding and feeling way too sterile," he interjected, shaking his head. "And I'm not liking it."

"Well—"

"This is supposed to be an interview where I'm supposed to tell my side," Luke cut in again. "At least that's how your editor and my AD explained it to me. There should be some level of comfortability between us so I can do that..."

I scoffed. Couldn't help it.

He folded his arms over his chest and leaned back in his seat. "You've got some kind of wall up, giving off the vibe like you're doing me a favor—"

"Because I am," I jumped in. "I'm doing you a favor. You need me."

He kissed his teeth. "Nah, I don't."

I blinked in response.

"I don't need anyone."

"When you're losing your shit on a university basketball court, you do—"

"Because Brookville U's coach lacked class and respect," he spat back. "Something I'm realizing might be a part of BU's university culture based on present alumna."

I gritted my teeth.

"*Whatever* the reason," I started again, "this interview is to benefit you."

"Doesn't feel like that right now," he countered. "Especially if I'm having to deal with your funky ass attitude."

"We're not old friends, Luke," I sneered. "Not in the least. But I have a job to do. So, let's muscle through this interview and move forward with our lives. *Please*."

"Nah." He shook his head. "No. It doesn't feel right and it ain't gelling. If that's supposed to be your job, you're not doing it well. I want someone else."

I jerked my head back. "Excuse me?"

"I want someone else," he maintained with more venom. "I'm

requesting someone else do this interview with me because you're coming into this whole thing hot and bothered with a gripe against me, and I don't like that."

"You don't like that," I parroted, narrowing my eyes at him. "Not you playing the victim."

He palmed, then raised his glass to his lips to sip.

"If there is one thing I am, Luke," I told him, "is a real ass bitch. I don't play pretend or politics. So fuck no. I'm not coming in here all effervescent willing to act all chummy, chummy with you when I don't fucking feel like it."

He clenched his jaw.

"We are *not* cool. Period. But I can still do my job. And this interview is bigger than you. So, let's just get through with this."

"You sound bitter, Juliette," he noted with a menacing smirk. "Like you're still hung up over that little *thing* that happened between us over a decade ago."

I gasped to myself and held onto the breath I inhaled in response, immediately feeling lightheaded. My first instinct after that was to reach across the table to slap the shit out of him.

For him to address the elephant in the room and, in a way that showed no remorse, was deliberately disrespectful.

At least it was to me.

Because there was nothing *little* about what happened between us. And it wasn't a *thing*. It was *something*. Something so powerful. Memories of that night's event still played on my mind like my favorite TV rerun. The kind with an ending I always wished I could change.

But at that moment, I let it go. All the things his comment made me feel, I let it go. I chose instead to release the breath I held and to inhale another *long* stream of air to remain calm.

"The world doesn't revolve around you, Luke," I countered in my exhale. "Contrary to what you might think, I don't give a shit about you."

Whew.

What a lie.

"Good evening," our cheery male server greeted when he approached our table. "Can I start you two off with something to drink?"

Luke and I maintained our death stares as the server waited for an answer. The tension was so palpable between us. The chefs in Mon Ami could cut Luke and my beef with each other using a butcher's knife and sear it on their kitchen's grill.

Luke moved his eyes off me to focus up at the server to ask, "Can you give us five more minutes?"

"Oh! Absolutely," the server obliged. "Take your time."

"I don't feel comfortable with you," Luke stated the moment we were alone again. "As I've already made clear - I want someone else."

I balled my lips together.

"I want someone else to conduct this interview, someone who is objective and doesn't hate me. That ain't you. *You* are not the one for *me*."

I didn't hate him.

And I know he was talking about the interview, but hearing those words from him hurt.

You are not the one for me.

It was like he *wasn't* referring to only the interview.

As if he'd decided I wasn't good enough for him.

Again.

I swallowed back the tears, pushing back the urge to cry, and closed my notepad.

Snatched up the voice recorder next and dropped both items back into my briefcase while sliding my chair back.

I didn't utter any parting words. Just as I'd entered, I planned to leave the same way.

Because I was truly done.

There was no way I would give Luke the satisfaction of me pretending everything was all good for his benefit when deep down there was a wound, unhealed, inflicted by him, and that ached in his presence.

So I stood to my feet and got up from the table, grabbed my wool cape off the chair and walked off, feeling worse than how I felt before I arrived.

* * *

I watched Manhattan appear as a motion blur of buildings flashing past my window. The yellow cab I rode in the backseat of whizzed down the blacktop road headed toward traffic. My driver turned onto a street to join a parade of vehicles at a red light, waiting to drive onto the Brooklyn Bridge.

The brief reunion and argument with Luke played in my mind repeatedly, like how a scratched vinyl record skipped audio on a turntable.

We were still arguing... in my head. Because I'd come up with five different comeback lines as I replayed his words to me after leaving Mon Ami. And I'd brainstormed five more while sitting in the back of the cab. All centered on what I should've said to Luke. Just in that backseat arguing with myself, rearranging my words so I felt like a victor walking out of the restaurant instead of a loser in love and a loser in my career since I didn't get the guy or the story.

"I should've thrown my glass of water in his face," I mumbled to myself.

It would've been childish and extremely immature, but at least I'd have something to show for being so pissed off.

I didn't have my interview, another journalist at FTC will get a shot at covering probably one of the biggest cover stories of For The Culture's brief history, and my chances of getting editor after today will diminish substantially.

When I tell Mykal I walked out of the interview with Luke, the news will disappoint her, but she couldn't be more disappointed in me than I was in myself.

I shut my eyes and dropped my head back against the leather seat, wanting the night to be over.

My phone vibrating in my wool cape pocket interrupted my sulking. When I pulled it out to check who was calling, the number was unfamiliar.

"Hello?"

"Juliette." His voice in my ear was a dangerous thing. "It's Luke."

"Uh..." I exhaled into the phone and shook my head quick to gather my thoughts, because, "How did you get my number?"

"I asked my AD to get it from your editor-in-chief yesterday, so I would have it in case I needed to reach out to you before the interview."

I'd never spoken to Luke on a phone before. If I did, I would've remembered. Because he had a commanding voice, you'd never want to hang up on. It was quiet storm deep and so fucking unfair for him to have in his possession.

Because he had everything else. Ugh!

"What do you want?"

I asked that softly, too softly. Breathy and without all the warlike energy I was giving less than half an hour ago.

Real ass bitch, my ass.

I rolled my eyes at the defeat in my voice.

"I'm sorry," he apologized. "For what I told you at the restaurant, for..." He breathed into the phone. "I'm sorry Juliette."

My cabbie entered the bridge's entrance behind a long line of cars. Even at the dark hour of 8pm, on a night where we could see our breaths in the air, pedestrians were still walking across the Brooklyn Bridge to my left.

"Are you still in the city?" He asked next.

"Maybe. Why?"

"I'd really like to try interviewing with you again."

"What happened to getting someone else to do it?"

"Juliette," he answered in a whisper, and even that sounded good on the phone. "Can you meet me halfway on this, please?"

I rolled my tongue around my mouth.

"Our night started in a less than ideal way, but it doesn't have to end the same."

"Okay, well, you could've avoided all of that if—"

"Juliette, can you chill?" he pleaded this time. "Please?"

I tucked my lips into my mouth to keep quiet.

"I know what I said to you, aight? And I know I could've avoided our back and forth at Mon Ami. Which is why *now,* I am *trying* to salvage a night I played a part in almost fucking up," he added. "Can you allow me some grace to do that? Please?"

I fought the smile pulling at the corners of my mouth because, my goodness. He sounded so good.

"I'm heading to NoHo Cigar Lounge on Broadway-Lafayette Street," he started. "I should be there in the next five minutes. If you're still interested in interviewing me, you can find me over there. Cool?"

"*Mmm-hmm,*" I answered. My attempt at not sounding so eager.

"Aight, cool. Later," he said low before ending the call.

I twisted my lips to one side to bite inside my cheek, thinking. Brooklyn was straight ahead, Manhattan now behind me. Beyond needing the interview, seeing Luke again after getting our first inter-action out of the way after not seeing each other for so long had me curious.

And excited, if I'm being honest.

What would it be like *this* time?

"Excuse me?" I tapped my nails on the plexiglass that served as a divider between the driver and the back seat. "Change of plans. Can we head back to Manhattan to the NoHo Cigar Lounge on Broadway-Lafayette Street?"

eight

NOHO CIGAR LOUNGE, NEW YORK,
NEW YORK – WEDNESDAY,
FEBRUARY 15, 2023

LUKE

I SAW her copper corkscrew curls before actually laying eyes on her... again.

Same thing happened at the hotel restaurant less than an hour ago.

Hair first, then eyes.

I wasn't sure if Juliette would accept my invite to the cigar lounge. Not after how we left things yet again. But I was following my friend Trey's helpful advice, hoping it would work.

"Luke, what is it?" Trey breathed into the phone.

That was the thing about my boy Trey. Regardless of when I called, he'd answer, and I was damn happy he didn't disappoint tonight.

"I think I fucked up, man."

Juliette had stormed out of the restaurant, Mon Ami, seconds prior.

The moment she was gone, I knew I didn't handle our meeting the way I imagined handling it in my head.

I immediately panicked.

"Juliette and I." I clenched my hand into a fist, pissed at myself. "We just got into a back and forth I think was unnecessary, but she stomped out of here and shit between us is even more unresolved."

"So... why the fuck you calling me and not her, Luke?!" He asked, as out of breath as he was when he answered. "I'm a little busy right now."

"What do you think I should do, man? What should I say when I call her? How do you suggest I fix it? I really need to fix this, Trey." I ran my palm down my lips, pulling on my beard hairs at their wiry ends. "Because beyond needing the interview for LU, I never realized how much I've missed her until tonight, which is crazy 'cause I barely know her, but I really loved seeing her again, and... shit. I sound so goddamn corny, fuck." I pinched the bridge of my nose. "I don't know what the hell I'm saying right now..."

"Well, if you don't know, I damn sure don't."

"Trey, get off the phone, baby." I heard a moan in the background. "And get back over here."

"Oh." I perked up in my seat. "Yo, are you... are you and Serenity—"

"Having sex?" He hissed. "Yes!"

"Aw, man, my bad." I clasped my hand to my lips. "Damn. Why'd you answer?!"

"Because my best friend was calling, and I thought it was an emergency."

I snorted. "You can send me to voicemail next time, you idiot. I'll be all right."

"Be yourself," he told me.

"What?"

"You asked what you should do and how you can fix whatever mess you created tonight with shorty, correct?" he reminded. "Be yourself. No hiding this time. No walls up. It's time to take off the armor, man, and quit choosing to fight with her. Instead, put down your guard with her. Forget all the shit everyone else has told you regarding how to be around women

you're attracted to and be the Luke everyone else knows. The man who is all heart and all passion. It's not weak or corny for a woman to see that side of you and know that about you. Just show her you, no masks, and if that doesn't work, then shit." He snickered. "Third time might not really be a charm for you two, bruh."

Be myself.

Sounded simple enough.

Inviting Juliette to NoHo Cigar Lounge in a busy neighborhood north of Houston Street, less than fifteen minutes from my home, seemed like the best way to do that.

Much like at the restaurant, I spotted Juliette the moment she entered the lounge. And much like the restaurant, the lounge had its own version of foot traffic.

This is the place I visited whenever I didn't want to sit home and smoke alone.

NoHo Cigar Lounge was smaller than the other cigar lounges in New York City. But what it lacked in size, it made up for in quality with their variety of cigars and spirits.

Outfitted in wood grain wall paneling the color of brown sugar cane and furnished in brown leather quilted armchairs, besides their cigars, cigar connoisseurs knew NoHo best for their all-wood bar lined with wall-to-wall bottles filled with high-end whiskey, cognac, rum and bourbon. This cigar lounge was perfect for me. It was quiet with warm lighting. Classic R&B and jazz instrumentals hummed from unseen speakers, serenading patrons. It was a place I could keep to myself. My home away from home, and an excellent representation of Luke Lockett now.

I didn't hold back my smile this time when Juliette walked closer to my reserved section in the lounge, relieved she accepted my invitation.

I knew the owner personally because of my frequent visits. As a gesture of appreciation for my patronizing his business, he told me to let him know whenever I planned to visit and he would reserve a section for me. And I've taken him up on his offer every time I visited.

"Hello," she greeted when close. Her eyes were scanning me and the surrounding area as she unbuttoned her designer wool cape.

"Thanks for coming," I said, standing to my feet to make my way to her, walking behind her to assist her in removing her cape.

She allowed me in her space to help.

"Thank you for extending the invitation," she said low, glancing over her shoulder to look at me. "Hopefully, the sequel to tonight is better."

Her copper curls smelled nice, like a garden of patchouli in late autumn, which was easy to notice with me being as close.

"I'm confident it will be," I told her, draping her cape over the neck of the leather quilted armchair. "I want to apologize again for earlier."

Juliette blinked her pretty eyes in response.

"I'm sincerely sorry, Juliette. My behavior earlier was uncalled for, juvenile, and not the way I like to do things."

Juliette arched a brow. "Not the way you like to do things?" She crossed her arms next. "That's surprising. Since when?"

"Aight, fine. I deserve that." I chuckled at her challenging me. "I'll correct myself. It's not the way I like to do things... *anymore*."

"Oh, okay." She bit back her smile. "Because I was about to say."

I brushed a hand down my beard to hide my humor. I was already feeling good again in her presence.

Juliette's eyes moved around the establishment some more. "What's definitely not juvenile is this place. Very grown and sexy. Not my usual setting for interviews, but it seems quiet enough. You come here often?"

"At least once a week."

"Hmph." She licked her thick lips, eyes landing on mine again to find me staring.

I rubbed my hands together and asked, "Ready to pick out a cigar?"

Her brows piqued as she pointed at herself. "Me? Oh, *umm*, I didn't *plan* to smoke?"

I smiled. "I think you know more than anyone how unreliable *plans* can be."

Juliette balled her lips and dropped her eyes to the hardwood floors. Her eyes met mine again when she admitted, "I've never smoked a cigar before."

"Great, 'cause I'm happy to coach you on how to smoke one."

She bit at her bottom lip nervously. "Luke—"

"We're not cool," I acknowledged. "I know."

"I would not say that—"

"Twice?"

She scoffed a laugh.

I ran my hand down my beard and took a step toward her. "I know our history is what it is, and I promise I'm not trying to act like how you feel after everything isn't valid, but... listen, this interview? It's important to LU. And I know you don't give a fuck about LU, but I do, okay?"

She folded her arms over her chest again.

"Now, what we're going to talk about tonight, ain't something little, feel me?" I took a breath to watch my tone, feeling myself get upset about the whole reason I was doing the interview. "It affected me, and I want to make sure we cover everything, so there are no more questions. I know me." I pressed my hand to my chest. "If I feel this shit is clinical, just protocol? I will not be comfortable. And if I'm not comfortable, I'm gonna miss some things and I want to lay everything out tonight regarding that incident, so I *never* have to talk about it again."

She parted her lips to speak, and I placed a hand on one of her folded arms to stop her. "I know you got your way of doing things, but I need you to do me a huge solid tonight, Juliette."

She blinked in response.

"I need you to adjust, baby. Let me lead." I gestured over my shoulder toward NoHo's humidor. "Let's take a walk to the humidor, where there are several boxes of cigars."

She glanced where I gestured, then refocused on me.

"I'll help you pick one out, teach you how to smoke it, and I will answer all questions you ask me here tonight and give you a bomb ass interview. Full transparency." I pressed my palms together. "You have my word."

A small smile pulled at her lips and that was all the confirmation I needed for us to proceed.

Although I kept cigars in my home for personal enjoyment, I never brought them to NoHo. As one of the few cigar lounges in the city, I supported the business entirely. Purchased their cigars, bought their drinks, and chilled in their lounge, buying things to support my stay as necessary.

Because Juliette had never smoked a cigar before, I opted to help her sort through the cigars rolled with milder tobacco, since those would be mellow and not as full-bodied as the cigars I preferred.

Her eyes widened in wonderment at all the boxes of cigars in the humidor. She inhaled the air and moaned a little in an exhale as she moved about the room of cigars surveying her choices.

It was a pleasure for me, watching her experience one of my loves for the first time. Completely immersed in choosing a cigar, glancing at me whenever she was unsure and fielding my insight.

She eventually chose a hand rolled MonteCristo cigar from the humidor and a glass of whiskey at the bar, since I suggested the two paired well with each other.

Then we were back at our reserved spot in the lounge, sitting across from one another.

A butane lighter, a sterling silver cigar cutter, and an ashtray decorated the center of the wooden table between us. To each of our rights on the table was the whiskey we ordered at the bar.

I cut the head of the cigar and handed the cigar to her, instructing her to, "Wet this end in your mouth."

She stared at me with beautiful brown eyes.

"Not too much, though." I gestured with the cigar, waiting for her to take it out of my hand. "Wet it enough so it doesn't unravel from being too dry between your lips."

Juliette finally accepted the cigar and did as advised. Her eyes stayed on mine during that short time, glossy, naturally pink lips wrapped around the width of the cigar. Her lips looked so sexy with a cigar between them.

"Good," I rasped, immediately clearing my throat to rid the lust in my voice. I extended my hand to the cigar again. "That should be good."

When her cigar was back in my hand, I held it at an angle to light the foot.

"When did you start smoking cigars?" She asked, observing.

"When I got drafted to play in Madrid," I answered, waving the flame from my handheld butane lighter around the foot of the cigar, toasting it, and watching as the flame glowed blue and yellow. "It became my hobby. Collecting cigars. Trying to identify the different tastes and aromas of each one."

"Cigars are popular in Spain?"

I glanced up at her for a moment to see her eyes fixed on my hands working.

"Very." I turned the cigar to examine the toasted end. "Spain is the largest market for Cuban cigars. They're also more affordable in Spain more than anywhere else. Here." I held her cigar out to her to take again. "You're going to put it back in your mouth and I'm going to light it again."

She nodded.

"As I light the cigar, you're going to puff the smoke in and out so we can get the cigar ignited."

She batted her lashes. "Do I inhale?"

"Never inhale, Juliette. We're not smoking weed."

She giggled. My eyes lowered to her lips in response, drawn to how her top lip curled a little when she laughed.

I licked my lips at that.

"We smoke cigars for their tastes and notes and..." I bit my bottom lip as I scooted forward in my seat and closer to her to light her cigar. "... it's the perfect way to relax, which you need to do."

She rolled her eyes as she puffed.

It only took another forty minutes for Juliette to do exactly that. To relax. From the moment she walked into the hotel restaurant earlier, I sensed her nervous energy.

At the lounge, though, she was more laid back. She got rid of the camel blazer she wore beneath her wool cape, draping both outerwear items in a nearby armchair, revealing a black crop top only inches above the matching leggings. The plump crease in the space where her hips met her thighs was exactly the distraction I liked.

"What's it like coaching at Langston after playing there?"

Juliette asked for my permission to record our conversations in the lounge. I agreed only because recording while talking seemed more natural than what she originally had planned.

"Like the opportunity of a lifetime."

She smiled. "How so?"

"I get to pay it forward." I reclined in my seat and puffed my cigar. "Balling for LU was rewarding on court and eventually off the court. I lived in another part of the world, traveled all over Europe. Tried to learn a new language, but they spoiled me out there with translators and most of the country speaking English too. It feels good to show my players what's possible and to build them up so they can go out there and top what I've already done after graduation."

"Did you like playing overseas?" She asked next.

"It was cool. I learned a lot about myself, grew even more. Got exposed to different cultures that played a role in changing my life."

"Why'd you come back?"

"Loneliness." I admitted. "I missed my family, my sisters, although they were the exact reason I wanted to play basketball overseas."

"What did they do?"

I locked eyes with her and she shifted in her seat.

"Off the record," I stated.

"Got you," Juliette acknowledged.

"They were getting in the way," I admitted. "A bit too controlling and overbearing. Became exhausting, constantly having them in my ear all the time. I moved out of my parents' house after my high school graduation, but had never felt like I was really on my own until I moved to Europe. Out there overseas? I could finally make my own decisions. Had no choice but to learn how to do things my way and on my terms."

"And then you returned." She gestured at the recorder. "Started as assistant coach at LU and moved your way up to head coach in a short time."

"*Mm-hmm.*" I ran my tongue along my top teeth. "That's how the story goes."

She smiled. "Langston has done very good this basketball season with you as head coach."

"They've been a *very* coachable team," I acknowledged through my puffs of smoke. "My team followed directions to a T all season. They work together as one unit, and they hold each other account-able. I couldn't ask for a better army."

"That's one thing I give Langston," she said, eyes pointing down on her notepad. "Camaraderie is a strong suit."

I lifted a brow. "Is that a compliment I hear coming from you?"

Juliette laughed, peeking up at me. "I can give credit when credit is due."

"Interesting." I lifted my ankle to rest on my opposite leg's knee. "I thought Brookville's rivalry rule was to deny Langston's greatness until the day you die."

"If it is." She shrugged a shoulder. "I must've missed that memo. I never really enjoyed following Brookville's strict rivalry handbook, anyway."

"*That's* even more interesting." I smirked. "I wonder why that is."

"This is your interview," she said, eyes down on her notepad. "Not mine."

I bit my bottom lip and smirked.

"But since we're already talking about Brookville." She looked at me again. "Let's get right to it. What happened last Saturday?"

I puffed my cigar and moaned to myself as I released the smoke through my mouth.

"Video recorded from several camera angles captures you shoving Brookville's men's basketball coach, Coach Salvatore, and angrily gesturing at him while needing to be held back by your assistant coach and a couple of your players."

I glided my tongue over the smooth surface of my teeth again and thought before I spoke again. It was important now more than ever I chose my words carefully.

"One of the valuable lessons I learned while living overseas is to never limit myself to anything," I started. "Even if I don't know how I'm going to get something I want, if I know I want it, I know I can figure out how to get it. Because at its finest of elements, I can attain everything I want with three things - time, in steps, and with action."

Juliette held her pen in the webbing of her two fingers. Eyes focused on only me as she waited patiently for me to continue.

"That's literally how I became head coach in a short time, as you put it. It wasn't my plan, but the way I moved, the decisions I made set me up to be at the right place and at the right time to assume a position that could not go to anyone else."

I licked my lips and smiled.

"And that shit right there? Pissed off the boys' club."

"What do you mean?" She asked.

I scoffed. "Come on, now. You know what I mean."

Juliette lifted, then dropped her shoulders. "I don't."

"You were at Brookville during Coach Salvatore's years coaching, right?"

"Yeah."

"How would you describe him?"

"This is not my interview—"

"It's mine, I know," I cut in. "And my question applies to my point, so can you answer it?"

She cleared her throat and glanced at her recorder in the middle of the table before leaning forward to press the stop button to end the recording.

"I *can't* answer it." She pointed at the tiny silver device. "Because what I say in response can't be on the recording."

"Why not?"

"Because I'm a journalist, Luke," she explained. "I'm supposed to be unbiased in my writing, and my opinions of Coach Salvatore are *very* exact and *not* very good. Not in the least."

"Because he's a racist piece of shit, right?"

She tilted her head to one side, her copper curls falling that way. Her eyes scanned my face for a beat before she leaned forward again to press record.

"What happened on Brookville's court *before* you shoved Coach Salvatore?"

"Now *that's* a good question." I took a puff of my cigar and tugged at the neck of my burgundy pullover hoodie, feeling pissed all over again but keeping calm. "The ref had been making crazy calls all night against my players and I'd let it slide off my back like water. My focus is getting my boys ready for the conference championship. So all this other bullshit, these games? They represent steps. Those games are only practice for the real thing. I don't want my team to rely on being selected in March by a selection committee." I jabbed my finger into the arm of the armchair I sat on to emphasize my words. "I want the automatic bid into the NCAA championship. I want to be one of the 32 college basketball teams who won their conference championship. That's my only goal for the Blackbirds. Period. And to make sure of that, I keep my ballers confident and skilled. I keep 'em ready so they don't gotta get ready. And that's what they were last Saturday. Ready." I confirmed. "And it showed. Because, as usual, we were kicking Brookville's ass and, per usual, Coach Salvatore wasn't happy watching it happen."

"How'd he show this that night?" She asked.

"With everything. I knew he was on some bullshit the moment I entered the arena." I sucked my teeth. "At the start of the game, I made it a point to walk over and greet him. It was my first game against Brookville as head coach. I've seen Coach Walters do it all the time, even when I was a player. It was customary, good sportsmanship. We were at their home. Coach Walters never liked Salvatore. Shit, I disliked Salvatore more than Coach Walters. But." I leaned forward. "I refused to be petty about it. The thing is, when I approached Coach Salvatore to shake his hand, he refused to, conveniently, when there were no cameras around. I didn't sweat it. It was whatever. Like I said, I've never liked him and I only walked over there to be polite."

Juliette nodded her understanding.

"So cool. The game starts, right? The ref is calling fouls, disqualifying shots when they were valid buckets. Just being a fucking hard ass like I ain't never seen before." I ran a hand down my lips. "And for me, it's not something that's gonna bother me. I'm no stranger to it. I've dealt with it too, balling for LU. But then I'm seeing the effect of the stupid fucking calls on my guys' confidence. And I couldn't have that. Confidence is a priority in our practice. In everything. That's the one thing I work on with them. Because with confidence, that shit? It's powerful. A superpower that will take them farther than they have ever imagined. Beyond any basketball court. But, shit, the ref is fucking with their confidence *hard*, so now *I* gotta say something when I see it's getting to my players' heads."

"Makes sense."

"That's what I thought. That's the only reason I approached the ref, with the lightest of energy, because I know me. I don't play that shit in no way, but I see the cameras. It's my first game against a rivalry team I used to play. I know everyone is watching. And I know I got a temper. So I ask the ref what his deal was. I point out he and I both know my young men are out here playing with their hearts and balling well but are getting hit with a crazy number of ridiculous fouls, so what's up?" I suck my teeth as I recall what happened next. "Coach Salvatore, the fool who didn't want to shake my mother-fucking hand, didn't want to say over two words to me at the start of the game, approaches to come tell me I'm new to this and to let the ref do his job. So I tell his ass to mind his business and to get the fuck out of my face. Verbatim."

Juliette fought back her smile, which made me smile before I was gritting my teeth again.

"I guess he didn't like that answer too much or maybe he thought it was an invitation to get closer because instead of creating space between us." I clenched my jaw. "Coach Salvatore not only gets closer, but he drapes his arm over my shoulder."

Juliette arches a brow.

"Then he tells me real casually I'll always be a *nigger* who dribbles a ball to him and never a real coach of anything."

Her jaw dropped. "He said what?!"

"He was mid-sentence, probably with more to say, but after I heard that hard -er come out his mouth, I snapped. Shoved him off me and he shoved me back. So I shoved him again this time much harder, and I was approaching for more but as you saw went viral, people jumped in to get between us so all you got from the video was me shoving him then me being held back and cussing him out. Y'all didn't get to see or *hear* any of what transpired before that."

I puffed my cigar again to regain my calm, blowing smoke from my lips. "And that was cool with me. Still is. I've always turned up on court, and I always get judged for it even though my outbursts, as random as they might seem, are reactions equal to the actions. I'm Isaac Newton's third law in human form. So, I didn't care. It didn't matter cameras or whatever capturing me lose my shit yet again were there because Salvatore stepped out of line, and I was more than ready to put him back in it. 'Cause he tried me in a room full of people thinking I would shut up this time and take it because now I had something more than a game to lose. My career. A reputation." I shook my head. "And if he could talk like that to me, I already knew what kind of abusive shit he was saying to his black players on that team before I received confirmation of my suspicions after everything went down. And I didn't like that shit either. A stance had to be taken. I had time that night. He went too fucking far and only went there because he believed there would be no repercussions." I peeked down at my cigar and looked up at her again. "But what he didn't know about *me* is I don't play that shit. Didn't tolerate it as a student and definitely not as a grown ass man. 'Cause I don't care who it is, where I am, or who's watching." I took another puff of my cigar. "While others may not want any problems, I do. Because, see me? I always want the fucking smoke. *All* of it."

I blew white smoke overhead and leaned back in my seat, releasing all the tension in my body, refocusing on Juliette to find her with a huge smile on her face.

She sighed, lowering her view to the notepad on her lap to write. "I'll have to tell the photographers before Friday to photograph you with a lit cigar because of what you said and the timing of *that* was so fucking iconic. It is definitely going in this article."

"Cool," I told her. "I trust you."

She looked up at me. We held our stares for a moment.

Time had been fantastic for her. It's crazy to watch someone mature in different iterations in their life while watching from a distance.

Juliette blinked away, turning to her leather briefcase. "I think I have everything I need. Of course, I'll need to reach out to Coach Salvatore to get a quote from that night's events. Knowing him, he won't give it because although I've never heard him use a racial epithet, his actions toward BU's players have always spoken loud and clear."

"Hmph," I huffed.

"But what you've given tonight is good." She informed. "It's great."

"Good to hear." I bit inside my bottom lip.

The sound in her voice was of someone preparing to leave. I

didn't like the feeling that came over me, knowing that yet again, this would be our last time seeing one another. What other reason would have us in each other's company again after tonight?

"My editor will be in touch with your AD—"

"You leaving me again tonight?"

She stopped shuffling around with her briefcase to glance my way. "Well, we're done with the interview."

"So that means you gotta go?" I leaned forward to rest my cigar on its tray.

I watched Juliette swallow hard and not reply.

I could hear Trey's voice echoing in my head to just be myself. Let down my guard, stop hiding, and be all heart.

So I did that, if for nothing else, to see what happened.

"I'd like it if you stayed, Juliette," I admitted. "But if you have to go—"

"I can stay." She pointed at me. "But the minute you piss me off..."

"I'll behave." I pressed a hand to my chest. "Promise."

She smiled. "Okay."

That one word from her lips will always be the sexiest thing she can say to me. And she didn't even know it.

"So." I leaned forward for my drink. "How have you been, Juliette?"

nine

JULIETTE

MY FIRST INSTINCT was to reply to his question with, "I've been good," and that wouldn't have been a lie. I *had* been good, so I thought. I was living in the city of my dreams, surrounded by great friends, working in a rewarding career where I felt supported and encouraged to grow. And I would see the proof of my growth by the end of the year.

I've been good.

But, "Maintaining," came from my mouth as a response instead.

"I see you've been *maintaining* well," Luke replied.

He was right. What he told me on the phone earlier was right. Not just diving into our interview was for the best. And I knew that. I always start with ice breakers to get the subjects of my interviews comfortable to talk with me. But I wanted to get everything done quickly with Luke, because...

"You made me nervous tonight," I admitted.

He sat up in his seat to give me more of his attention.

"And I haven't felt that nervous feeling in a *long* time."

"Is that a good or bad thing?"

"It was a horrible thing." I crossed my legs in my seat, then my arms. "In your case."

He laughed. "Well, damn."

"Just being honest." I offered a blank gaze. "The last time I saw you—"

"Was not the way I should've let you leave my car," he interjected, dropping his forehead into his hand and scoffing a laugh. "What I did was wrong."

"What you did was fucked up, Luke," I corrected.

"What I did was fucked up," he echoed. "I shouldn't have said that to you, although I meant every word."

I blinked hard. "Excuse me?"

He licked the corner of his mouth and what a sight that was. I prayed he didn't piss me off because then I would have no choice but to storm out again and just, based on principle, I won't let myself return this time.

"I meant what I said," he doubled down. "I didn't want to be anyone's baby daddy." He lifted and dropped his shoulders. "I still don't. And I didn't want that kind of relationship with you either, not because you weren't dope, but because... I just didn't. Now how I went about telling you that was wrong of me, I'll admit. I should've explained myself but, Juliette." He fixed his eyes on me. "I meant that shit."

I looked away, focusing on the neutral browns in the lounge's decor and views of Manhattan from the oversized glass windows.

"What we did that night," he continued, "Have sex raw like that? I'd never done that with any other girl. Before you or after."

He licked his lips.

"I've always been careful. If there's one thing my father and my coach drilled into my head, it was condoms always. No exceptions." He rubbed his fingertips together. "I did nothing stupid like that. Never until that night."

"And you think I was running around fucking guys with no condom, Luke? Like? Come on. That's a little offensive." I chimed in. "And how do you think I felt after doing something I don't normally do and having the guy I did that with behave like he wished he never knew me?"

He closed his eyes and held them tight before brushing his hand down his beard slow. "Juliette—"

"I found what you said to be cold and downright heartless." I ran my fingers through my curls. "And I'm glad you explained what you meant, but back then? What you said left me feeling so hurt and insecure."

I held a hand up.

"And I'll admit, I wasn't the most confident girl around guys at BU. Fine." I laughed nervously. "And I know it wasn't your responsibility to build that confidence in me, but for a short while after that night with you, my anxiety with guys grew insanely worse. I was so unsure of myself."

Luke was so tuned in, it seemed like he was listening to me with every part of his body as he sat straight in his seat hanging on to my every word.

"I don't know about you, but I never felt the things I felt with you that night with anybody else." I closed my eyes to hide a little from him, since admitting that to him made me feel so naked. "Those feelings, the sensations, they were so new to me and so different." I ran my fingertips along my brows. "I believed the reason you were so distant the day after was because I weirded you out."

He jerked his head back. "Weirded me out how?"

"When I... when we were..." I cleared my throat and laughed nervously. "My reactions when we were doing it—"

"What? No, Juliette." He shook his head slowly. "You thought you weirded me out?!"

"Yes."

"Damn." He chuckled. "That was the furthest thing from the truth. I swear to God on that."

"Well…" I snorted a laugh. "I had no actual way of knowing that since you wouldn't even look at me the day after Luke."

"I'm sorry, Juliette." Luke scooted to the edge of his seat and reached across the coffee table, taking my hand in his. He pressed his free hand to his chest and told me. "I'm sorry. It was selfish of me to think of only myself that day and to be so careless with your feelings. It was wrong of me, it was cowardly, and it was entirely my bad. I am *so* sorry. For real."

His apology made me release a long, relieving breath. Luke's words were sincere as he looked me right in the eyes and decreed each word. The only place they could have come from was his heart.

My hand was still in his when he added, "I felt nothing like what I felt with you that night either, and I'm not talking about just the experience. I mean… don't get it twisted. That night with you was…" He blew air through his lips. "More than anything I could ever put in words. But I'm talking about my confusion with *why* I did it *the way* we did it more than anything else. You frightened the shit out of me. And your reactions while we were intimate weren't what scared me. *You* scared me because of what I did *with* you. I didn't want to talk because I was scared. You made me want to do things I didn't think I knew how to do. I was dealing with feelings I couldn't figure out how to process. Thoughts bogged my mind down with trying to under-stand what it was about you that made me want to risk it all. You were beautiful, still are, but goddamn, Juliette." He laughed. "You humbled me. You also made me think you put some kind of voodoo on me that night to make me do something I knew better not to do."

I cracked a smile.

His fingers caressed the skin on the back of my hand. "It was my choice to have sex raw, I know that. But back then, my view on girls my age was a negative one, and I was stuck trying to figure out what about this girl named Juliette made me want to go through with having sex with her without protection and why I wasn't regretting it afterwards."

He gently let go of my hand to recline back in his seat.

"So much could've happened after that night." He picked up his glass of whiskey and took a sip. "So much we weren't ready to deal with had they happened. And just those thoughts, only the thoughts, scared the shit out of me."

"You're right," I agreed. "A lot could've happened."

Silence settled between us for a bit. He balanced his drink on his denim knee.

"And for the record," he said to me. "What you showed me that night was too beautiful and way too pure for me to *ever* be weirded out by it, aight?" He bit his bottom lip. "It remains the most stunning thing I've ever seen in my life."

I tried to fight my smile, but I didn't stand a chance after hearing that.

"And I've seen some dope ass shit. The Eiffel Tower, the Sistine Chapel ceiling, and the inside of an Egyptian pyramid, to name a selected few, and baby." He moaned low. "None of them can compete because none of them compare. I have yet to see a sight more beautiful than the faces you made with me inside you."

I looked away shyly, trying my damndest not to melt into the leather seat beneath me.

"Well, since we're being honest..."

"*Mm-hmm...?*" He encouraged.

"You haven't seen a sight since me and I haven't found a better feeling since you." I admitted. "I've been damn near chasing the feeling ever since Kaysville."

"Sounds exhausting." He smirked behind the rim of his glass.

I rolled my eyes, and that made him laugh.

"So, does this mean you're single?" he asked next.

"I am," I confirmed. "You?"

"Very," he answered.

"Shocking."

"I could say the same for you." He chuckled. "What's your baggage?"

"My what?"

"Your baggage," he repeated. "What's keeping you single?"

"Nothing." I lied. "I don't have any baggage."

"We all got baggage, Juliette." He leaned forward to set his drink on the coffee table.

"I mean, if anything, my baggage is not getting over a one-night stand I had in a small town called Kaysville my senior year in college."

"Oh, come on," he uttered in response.

"I'm serious," I said. "You ruined me, for real."

"Impossible," he said low. "You're perfect."

I sputtered a laugh. "Luke, *please*. You barely know me."

"I know enough to know that." He held up a finger. "And I feel that way even though your alma mater is a school I *absolutely* despise. But I'm sure you feel the same way about Langston—"

"I don't," I admitted, shaking my head.

He looked at me, his brows wrinkled.

"I *love* Langston."

Those same brows shot up fast in reaction. "I'm sorry, what?"

"I. Love. Langston U," I repeated slowly. "Always have. Langston University was my first choice when I was applying to universities in high school."

"Get the fuck out of here!" His voice echoed around us.

I tossed my head back in a laugh.

Luke scooted to the edge of his seat quickly. "You're fucking with me, right?"

I shook my head. "Nope."

"Wait, wait, wait." He waved a hand in the air. "What are you telling me right now, Juliette?!"

"I've always wanted to study at LU. I wanted to go to Langston the day I saw the campus from the backseat of my parents' silver Mercedes at 12-years-old." I smiled. "They were handling business at one of their cleaners in the city and had to take a detour because of street closures. One of those detours had us driving down 1 University Plaza."

"Langston's block," he smiled back, knowingly.

"*Mm-hmm.*" I closed my eyes to reminisce. "God, it was so beautiful. Right there in Manhattan, surrounded by all those skyscrapers. Big ol' lawn with gorgeously built campus buildings. I saw one game on ESPN during the conference tournament and saw the Ravens in action and that was all it took for me to fall in love with LU. The Ravens were the reason I joined my high school's cheerleading squad, just so I could be ready when it was time to join stomp and cheer." I snickered. "I just *knew* Langston would be where I would go to college by the time I was 13-years-old and when it came time to apply during the fall of my senior year in high school, my parents were not for it at all."

"Why not?"

"Though they liked to make their money in New York's boroughs, they weren't comfortable with me going to school there." I twisted my lips to one side. "They watched the news a lot. To them, the city was full of muggings, terrorist attacks, and assaults on young women. Manhattan was too dangerous, especially for their only daughter. They forbade it. Told me flat out no and to pick another school. I was an enormous people pleaser back then and respected their wishes. Picked a school that was close to home so they'd be happy."

"Brookville."

I nodded.

"They loved it when we did the campus tour my senior year in high school. The town of Brookville looked a lot like where we lived. Small town, surrounded by a bunch of farms, and high schools the size of college campuses." I kissed my teeth. "The more I saw what Brookville University had and what they offered, the more I wanted to go to Langston. I wanted the city so badly. I wanted the subways, the street food, the 24hr convenience stores, lit up nights. I wanted Manhattan. But." I shrugged. "They were paying for it and I didn't think it would matter much. It was just college. So, I settled for BU."

"I thought you were at BU because you *wanted* to be at BU."

"Puh-lease." I laughed. "I couldn't wait until I finished serving my time there. I couldn't say that, though. It isn't BU Lions pride. My friends I made there were the *only* reason I stuck it out and didn't quit school."

He cracked up laughing. "So you're telling me we could've met for the first time on LU's campus? Better yet, at freshman orientation?"

"Luke." I laughed again. "You and I both know you wouldn't have noticed me."

"I would've."

"You were a big deal before you even stepped on LU's campus," I recalled. "You had a whole press conference announcing what university you would go to, I later learned. *Everyone* knew who you were prior to you playing your first game. Faculty and students at Brookville U knew your name, and you weren't even a student at my school. And then there was me." I laughed. "*Just* Juliette Hart."

"On God?" He said. "I would've noticed you, *just* Juliette Hart."

His voice was firm.

Decided.

Unyielding.

And did the job of shutting me the hell up.

"All those big copper curls of yours?" He smiled. "It would've been hard as hell to keep my eyes off you."

"I bet." I snorted. "I love my hair now. But being a red headed black girl was my biggest insecurity as a child. I used to beg my parents to dye it black so the other kids would stop teasing me, which my parents refused to do—"

"I would've refused, too," he cut in. "Your hair is so damn beautiful, Juliette. Like, really, really beautiful."

I blushed.

"It's one of my favorite things about you." Luke's eyes softened when he added, "And there are *a lot* of things I find interesting about you. So I know for sure I wouldn't have been able to see anyone else at LU once I saw you. I know that for a fact."

Soft jazz instrumentals filled the brief silence between us.

"This whole time I thought you were like everybody else over there at BU," he continued. "But now you're telling me LU was where you wanted to be? Damn." Luke brushed his hand down his beard.

"I told you I wasn't like them," I reminded.

"You did, but…" He shook his head and mused that, "My perception of you was all wrong."

His eyes moved off mine, lowering down my form in a visual perusal I swore I could feel.

"Come home with me tonight, Juliette," he said next, meeting his eyes with mine again.

The invitation was such a surprise. My breathing hitched the second he extended it to me.

I was moving my eyes off him when he added, "Please don't think about it."

I locked eyes with him again.

"Just." He made a shrugging motion with the sides of his mouth. "Baby, just say… okay."

That one word for us was more than a simple four-letter word. It held weight. Dripping with so much intent. Interesting things have happened when I've uttered that word and my curious ass wanted to see what more could come from me saying it.

I nodded. "Okay."

* * *

The first thing I noticed when I walked into Luke's place behind him was how much it smelled like him.

It was a pleasure to discover exactly what that mystery scent was I smelled on him at the hotel restaurant earlier.

Cigars.

The smoky, spicy, earthy aroma mingled well with his cologne to create a signature scent that was so grown and sexy, and painstakingly alluring.

That's what lingered in the air in his condo, beckoning me over the front door's threshold.

I inhaled a lung full of it as I strutted past his kitchen and entered his living room. The space was small, slightly larger than mine, and with masculine minimalist vibes everywhere, even in the rare oil paintings adorning his white walls.

Floor-to-ceiling windows straight ahead of me sparkled in the reflection of lights from neighboring buildings, including the Freedom Tower in the distance. To the right of Manhattan's buildings was a view of the Hudson River.

The palm plant thriving at the side of his bedroom entrance surprised me. It also surprised me to see a plant on the natural stone island that divided the kitchen from the living room. I spun around to see Luke leaning on his bedroom door frame outside of his room, watching me appraise his condo.

He still wore his wool camel trench over his burgundy hoodie, blue jeans, and color coordinating Jordan Ones.

If someone told me I would end my night at Luke Lockett's place when I got up that morning, I wouldn't have believed them.

But here I was.

Here *we* were.

And that fact was blaring in my mind like an emergency siren.

"This is exactly how I would expect your place to look," I told him. "Minus the plants."

Just like him, I hadn't removed a single article of clothing, not even my hooded Burberry cape.

I knew why he invited me to his home. The idea alone was intriguing, and maybe my curiosity motivated me to accept.

"*Why* minus the plants?"

"Never took you for a plant guy, is all." I glanced at them, then focused on him again. "Why do you have them?"

"I enjoy having living things around me to nurture and care for," he revealed easily, sliding his hands into his jeans pockets.

I sighed at that. Intrigued even more by a guy I thought I knew, but may have been as wrong about him as he was about me.

"And how does my place look?" he asked next.

Luke Lockett's appeal as a 21-year-old young man was very unfair. He had the deep raspy voice, with eyes that made him easy to trust, lips that looked like a pleasure to kiss, and a height that looked fun to climb.

But Luke Lockett's appeal as a 32-year-old single man felt like a lethal weapon.

He still had all those same qualities, but now those qualities had matured. Time and his life experiences after college had refined him. Now he was patient, too. And that was magnetic. I knew why I was there, but he hadn't hinted at it, nor had he given any sign confirming that was the reason I was actually there.

The man had removed nothing since we arrived.

"Comfy," I remarked low. "It looks stylish and comfortable in here."

He glanced around himself at his space.

When Luke's eyes returned to me, this time I found the heat in his gaze. There when he lowered his eyes from mine to examine my neck, then the rest of my body.

My heart gradually picked up in rhythm. The feeling was one I hadn't felt in a while. A long while. Other guys hadn't been able to give me the knotting in my stomach or that lightheadedness. The ache between my thighs forcing me to shift off one leg and onto another to soothe it. A tension in me that builds and is palpable, and anyone else would probably find the whole thing to be uncomfortable, but it gave me quite the thrill.

Luke pushed himself off the doorjamb and made his way over to me in slow strides to his living room. He brought with him his cologne and a pocket of air that allowed his scent to reach me before he did.

I released a trembling breath because let's be honest here. Not that long ago, in the night, I was nervous about only sitting and talking with this man and now we were about to do more than talk. After I promised myself I wouldn't let another man get too close to me again.

Shouldn't that apply to him the very most, since he was the catalyst for that promise to me?

Should I have accepted his invitation to come here?

He seemed different, though. Instead of letting me storm out of his life again, he called me and apologized. But I couldn't shake this fear of history repeating itself with us somehow.

Because what would make this time different from the other one?

I didn't have the answers to any of what confused me, so the questions festered, and that shit caused uncertainty. Made me feel like being there probably wasn't the best idea.

I looked around me again.

Looked around at where I was.

In Luke's home... after all *that*.

The surrealism was fucking with me and not in the way I would've liked.

A sudden wave of self-doubt drowned me in more questions, killing my vibe. I couldn't shake feeling stupid for being there with him, of all places.

He got me to his condo with only six words.

Come home with me tonight, Juliette.

Was I that easy?

I glanced at his front door, considering how to leave.

"Juliette," he said calmly.

I looked towards his voice.

We held our stares.

"What are you thinking, Juliette?"

I shook my head.

"Tell me what you're thinking, baby."

"I'm thinking..." I pinched the bridge of my nose. "I'm thinking I shouldn't be here. That I've made this too easy for you to have access to me again after all these years."

"Nothing about tonight has been easy," he said, eyes moving along my face, analyzing as he spoke. "Not for you, not for me."

Luke walked closer, more in my space, taking my hand.

"I admire you," he started. "And how easily you share what you're feeling. You wear your emotions on your face, so there's never a mystery what's on your heart. At least not to me."

I half smiled. "It's a gift and a curse."

"It's one of my other favorite things about you."

"You don't even know me, Luke."

"But I know I love that."

I blinked in response.

"Maybe because I'm not as easy to read, and that can pose as a challenge, leaving people unsure about me. Uncertain of my intentions." He ran the pad of his thumb over my knuckles, and I warmed right up. "And I rarely care, but I do with you. I want you to know exactly what's on my mind. I need a little patience from you, though, Juliette, as I get comfortable speaking to you from my heart."

My name on his lips each time he spoke it made the walls inside me contract.

He dropped his view into my hands. "I want to work on communicating my thoughts and my feelings with you more fluidly tonight, instead of keeping them to myself. But I've been on guard for so long it's probably a part of my DNA now. So it's gonna take some unlearning, aight?"

Luke laced his fingers with mine, using our connection to pull me more into his space, and I exhaled all the tension I held inside me, inhaling his scent again when I needed the air to breathe.

He was so intoxicating, I was certain I was getting high off him, standing this close.

His hand pressed into my lower back, bringing me closer. "I don't want you to leave because I don't want this night to end with you being anywhere else but here with me."

A soft moan escaped my lips.

"But if you don't want to stay, I'll respect your choice." He released my hand and walked behind me, moving my hair off my neck as he did. "Because I want you to *want* to stay just as much as I want you to."

"I want to stay," I whispered into the air.

Luke dipped his chin enough to brush his lips against my neck, not yet kissing me there. More like running the fullest parts of his mouth against my skin, heating the area while chipping at my resistance.

"Can I kiss you here?" he asked with a hand at the neck of my cape.

"Yes."

"Can I kiss you anywhere?"

"You can kiss me wherever your lips can reach," I whispered.

"*Mmm*," he moaned so deeply it resonated in my chest as he removed the cape. "Thank you."

Every slight touch he did against my body made my walls spasm between my thighs.

"You never asked me what my baggage was," he reminded.

I swallowed hard.

"It's that I've never gotten over you. I never stood a chance after you got a hold of me in that small town of Kaysville." As he worked on unbuttoning my blazer next, he revealed, "You said I ruined you? Well, you spoiled me. Because just like you, I've been chasing too, baby. But I haven't been chasing the feeling. It has always been the look for me."

I leaned the back of my head against his chest when he moved my blazer's sleeves down my arms.

"Your expressions," he moaned low in my ear, brushing his soft lips along the maze. "The night I witnessed your expressions while coming mesmerized me."

He guided fingers down the faux leather fabric of my leggings, gliding over the area where my pussy throbbed for his touch.

"I swear," he said to me, "I've been chasing that light you had in your eyes, on your face that night, trying like hell to replicate it in other women with no success. Your trust in me? How vulnerable you were with me inside you?" He lifted his hands high enough to slide into the band of my leggings. "That *need* that made me believe only I could meet? It was exhilarating, Juliette. So hypnotic, I refused to even blink, concerned I'd miss something if I did."

His fingers slid right into wetness and we moaned together when his fingertips found warmth to glide into.

"You were *so* soft to me that night, Juliette, and I just knew my ass was in trouble the moment I touched you just like this against that motel wall..."

"Luke," I whispered, biting my bottom lip.

"... and I swore I'd go through hell and high water to protect all you gave me in that motel room later that night, but baby..." He circled my clit with two fingertips. "I thought I wasn't ready for what came after that."

I tucked my lips in my mouth, leaning my weight back against him and he massaged my pink ball, nice and slow, using his free hand to hold me up.

"I was supposed to drive the Suburban the night I ran into you in BU's parking lot," he revealed in my ear as he strummed. "The plan was not for me to leave the truck. But I'd left my driver's license in my room, so we had to switch up our plans when we arrived at your school."

I placed a hand on top of his.

"And I wasn't supposed to be in front of Langston the night you walked out to see your team left," he breathed heavily in response to my exhales. "I was so tired after the game, but I wanted to get a slice of pizza from the pizzeria a block from campus. That's where I was going when I saw you standing outside of my school with a dead phone. And now, we meet again, Juliette." He pushed his hand further into my leggings to slide two fingers inside me. "And in the unlikeliest of ways yet again. Different iterations and scenarios, but all of them doing the same thing, putting us in the same place repeatedly? It just has to mean something. It has to be for a reason, you know?"

I moaned at the heat he stirred up in me. Hearing and feeling his words and his touch. I was about to burst from it all.

"There's something very strong, more powerful than the two of us that keeps pulling me to you and you to me." My knees buckled, and he groaned in my ear, holding me closer. "And I don't know what it is, but I don't want to doubt it anymore. I'm just so tired of wasting years I can't get back trying to figure out what that was between us in Kaysville. What this is between us now? I want to *know* this time. I'm so ready to find out now, Juliette."

I turned in his arms and threw my arms around him. Balanced myself on the arches of my knee-high boots and kissed him.

"I've missed you so much," he said on my lips, then parted them with his and searched for my tongue, lifting me off my feet to walk me out of his living room.

His bedroom floor is where the rest of my clothes laid beside his after I removed them in haste. Under gold cove lighting and on his California king, I stood between his splayed legs as Luke idled at the foot of the bed naked and only wearing a condom on his hard-on.

"Hold on one moment." is how he got me to stand before him completely naked. "Let me marvel and enjoy this beautiful view of you for a little."

His big hands caressed my hips and thighs. For what felt like a while, we held our stares as he massaged my skin. Luke broke eye contact only when his hands glided over flesh and curves. He visually feasted on my nudity in silence. Dragged trimmed nails over the fullest parts of my ass, used his grip on me to draw me closer to his lips so he could kiss me from my stomach to my landing strip.

He pulled me closer, lifted my leg by the nook behind my knee, resting it on his left shoulder blade. Luke took me by my hips and held me by the ass and guided me to his mouth. He tilted his head just right so he could use his lips to spread my lower lips apart to help himself to a taste of me.

He angled his head and used only his tongue to deliver feathered strokes against my clit, eyes focused up to watch me react. I was all breath at first, then soft moans. Then, with quaking legs and a racing pulse, I just had to let my head drop back and between my shoulders. There was no way I'd be able to remain on one foot with the mounting pleasure and sensual circles he created with only his wet tongue.

Aware of this, Luke lifted me up and off my feet, repositioning me flat on his bed. Between my thighs again, he circled his head and his tongue in quick succession, barely coming up for air. He only stopped after I arched my neck to brace myself as he licked me through a pussy pulsing orgasm.

He offered no break after. As I laid there trying to catch my breath, he kissed his way up my body and pressed his hand to his headboard and his free hand lightly against my stomach as he slid his hard into my soft. He kept his eyes locked on me and buried himself inside me to the root.

His strokes were shallow, controlled, and very deliberate. It all overwhelmed me. The sincere look in his eyes, the raw feelings between us, his dark skin reflecting the gold light in the room. It was too much for me to last through. I slid my hand between the gaps in his arms to lay my palms against his backside. I wanted to feel every-thing. His thrusts, his gluteal muscles, and his hips active. I couldn't help but to watch him through my heavy lids. Lean muscles flexing with his movements. Flecks of light shimmering in his beard. His jaw tensed each time my walls twitched from the friction him sliding in and out caused.

"You are so beautiful," came out of my mouth as a whisper.

"Nah, baby, that's you." His top lip curled into a sexy smile. "You must be seeing the reflection of yourself in my eyes."

His strokes faltered to a stop when I pressed my hands on either sides of his face.

"I'm serious, Luke," I swore. "What I see in your eyes are all the things you said you wanted me to see, and it's so beautiful."

He lowered his lips to mine to whisper against them, "And only for your eyes to see," before he parted them to stroke my tongue with his. His strokes between my thighs resumed, and he delivered them even slower than when we first started, but this time he dove deeper than before.

He put his face in the pillow beneath my head after breaking our kiss. I closed my eyes and held my lids tight, rocking under him, overwhelmed with so many emotions. I just had to let them out.

"I had the biggest crush on you, Luke," I confessed.

"Oh, I know." He chuckled lazily into my ear. "I had a crush on you, too."

His lips pressed into my neck, his warm breath from his exhales tickled me there a little as he sucked the skin into his mouth.

"I used to masturbate to thoughts of you at night after watching you play at BU's home games."

"Juliette, *shhh*." He groaned against me. "Don't tell me that right now, baby. I cannot hear you say that right now and not come quick."

"And I hated how bad I wanted you inside me," I confessed, my toes curling. "Because I was supposed to not like you and I thought I could never have you."

"You could've *always* had me," he promised in my ear.

My walls did that thing and my body responded to the action by trembling.

I squeezed each of his cheeks in my hands and held on as he pushed more of himself inside of me.

He was up on his hands and over me again, moaning when I moaned like we were enjoying and sharing in the same pleasure.

"I swear you could have anything you want from me when you make me feel like this," I admitted.

He chuckled sexily and said, "Same baby," as he pushed my legs back, using his forearms against my thighs.

My back arched in response.

I gyrated my hips slow beneath him, meeting his strokes each time he thrusted forward so he'd impale me more.

I wanted every inch of him.

"Shit," he groaned out. "You fucking me back like you want something from me *right now,* though, Juliette?"

Luke pressed his forehead to mine. "Am I right? You want something from me, baby?"

"Yes."

My hands fell to my sides as I gave in to his force, willingly leaving myself open to whatever.

"*Mmm,* what you want, baby?" He thrusted slowly, then fast, slowing it down again before repeating the pattern. "What you want from me, Juliette?"

And there was nothing to fear, no hang-ups to get over. I'd seen all I needed to see, and Luke was right. Something more powerful than us kept drawing us together, and I no longer wanted to fight it.

"You," I whispered, arching my back, releasing all the tension inside me. "I want all of you."

My jaw slacked, and he slacked his too. I was staring so long into his eyes my vision became blurry. I couldn't control anything after that, not even my eyes from rolling. Like I've always remembered happening with only him.

"*Mmm-hmmmm,* there it goes." he whispered through ragged exhales. "The most beautiful view in the world,"

I whimpered and moaned until I couldn't do either of those things, but yield to the pressure, then the gradually curling wave of coming beneath him. Rolled my head slowly left and right against the pillow under me, trying to ground myself because breathing became a task I couldn't complete. It overwhelmed me, feeling what I felt. I felt him so deeply, beyond penetration. I blinked and tears spilled out of my eyes, rolling down my cheeks. I was coasting through nirvana, on a natural high, just off the feeling.

"I wish you could see what I see, Juliette," he breathed over me. "You're really like no other, baby."

He pumped his hips, and I matched it all.

My eyes opened just in time to watch him come undone, too.

"You're so incredible," he whispered the second our eyes met. I pressed my fingers to his lips, and he kissed them before I lowered my hand to his back. He bared his teeth to inhale and exhale stuttered breaths through them. Luke grunted and groaned to the rhythm of his pelvis slapping with mine. I slid my hand up his back and caressed his spine, feeling his muscles tense and his body shudder against mine. He grew hard between my walls and uttered more curse words as whispers until he folded his lips in his mouth and bit them closed. Watching him went from being arousing to my body, reacting and trembling with his. I rolled my eyes closed and rocked with him, wanting to slow down time and lose myself in it all so the moment never ended.

I clung to him to anchor myself because I swore I'd float off the bed if I didn't. And when it was all done, he collapsed against me, dropping his head against my breasts. His weight on me paired with his heavy exhales brushing against my nipples stirred something new inside me.

I wanted more... *so* much more.

But for now, all we could do was catch our breaths together.

Luke rolled off me, landing on the pillow next to me. We were silent for a short while. Only our breathing doing the talking.

"Then I'm yours, aight?" Luke panted, turning to me. "You said you want all of me and I damn sure want all of you. Definitely more than *this*."

I snickered to myself, too tired to open my eyes. The man was for sure an athlete because how he found the energy to talk after blowing my mind was as impressive as his performance that night.

"Man, I'm just... I'm just so fucking grateful we've found our way back to each other, Juliette," he told me out of breath. "And I want you beyond this moment, even though this moment right now with you on my bed is *everything*."

I smiled to myself. He was a man of his word, communicating his thoughts and leaving nothing a mystery. I was finally in his head and it was more beautiful than I'd ever imagined.

He turned my face by my chin for me to look his way, and I found the strength to open my eyes to his.

"I'm yours if you want me." He smirked, running the pad of his thumb against my chin. "Aight, baby?"

I moved closer to him, only stopping when our lips touched again. On them, I responded affirmatively with, "And I'm yours."

LUKE

I CLOSED my binder of plays when my phone buzzed with a text. A quick glimpse at the device's screen showed me Juliette's name in a text bubble.

Juliette: I'll be there in 15mins

Me: Can't wait

I balled my lips to hold back my smile as I returned my device to my desk.

These last eight weeks have been nothing short of incredible. I've had to force myself to chill out with her because I wanted to take up all her time.

It was hard finding the hours in the day to do that, though, while preparing for and playing conference games.

I'd never been so stressed out as I was in March.

Juliette was an excellent support system during that time. I mean, I had my family there to do what they've always done, pour into me when doubt tried to fuck with my confidence. But there were some things relatives couldn't do for me that Juliette excelled at.

And God, did she excel at it.

I licked my lips, thinking about her.

Langston U's Blackbirds won our conference championship game receiving the automatic bid into March Madness.

You couldn't tell me shit that week. I was on cloud nine.

My team made it all the way to the fifth round in March Madness, the Final Four, but we lost by only three points, disqualifying us from playing in the National Championship Game. But that was okay. There was always next year. And next year, we'd bring the NCAA championship trophy home to New York City. That's my word.

The Blackbirds played a good game, and we did our thing. For my first year as head coach, making history as the youngest coach in the university's existence, winning our conference's championship and getting my players all the way to Final Four, had me feeling damn good about life.

My team winning our conference championship gave my family a reason to host a celebratory dinner in my honor.

I thought it would be a great time to invite Juliette to meet them.

We'd only been seeing each other for three weeks around that time, but I wasn't trying to wait. I wanted my family to know all about her.

"So, uh." I cleared my throat to get her attention.

We were at The Liquor Shop, a black owned bakery near to Juliette's studio co-op. It was a few days after the conference championship win and the dinner was the next day at my parents' home.

Juliette had been telling me about this bakery that infused their cupcakes, birthday cakes, and cake pops with wines and spirits. So that's where we were after spending her entire day-off in her bed.

Juliette moved her eyes off her yellow cake with white rum buttercream frosting to look up at me.

"My family is hosting a dinner to celebrate the conference championship win tomorrow night out here in Brooklyn." I rubbed my lips together. "Everybody's gonna be there."

She laid her plastic fork against the rim of the cake's clear container and tilted her head to one side.

I cleared my throat again. "My friends will be there, my sisters and my parents are gonna be there too..."

Juliette tried to fight back her smile.

"I was thinking, if you wanted to, you could... umm... you know, you could—"

"Be there," she finished with a smile.

I scoffed a laugh.

Her smile grew bigger, and I wanted to kiss it off her face.

"Lukeee," she crooned, wiggling her brows.

I pointed. "Do not start with that shit."

She tossed her head back in a laugh, her shiny copper curls bouncing in the air.

"See, I knew you would do this, man."

"You want me to meet your whole family? Wow!" She stuck out her tongue. "You think I'm special, huh?"

I kissed my teeth.

"You can say it." She bumped her shoulder against my arm. "You can tell me."

I turned away.

"Aht! Aht!" Juliette pointed up at me. "Remember what you told me."

"Here we go."

"I want to work on communicating my thoughts..." she teased in a faux deep voice.

I cracked up laughing. "Stop it."

"... and my feelings with you more fluidly," she finished.

"Okay, aight." I submitted, smiling. "I said it. I said that."

I wrapped an arm around her and pulled her to me, tilting her head back by her chin so she'd look up at me. "I want you to meet my whole family because you're special to me. You are very special to me, Juliette, and I mean that, baby. All jokes aside."

Her light brown skin reddened around her cheeks.

"And I want to tell the world about us, but I must start with the people closest to me. So it would mean a lot to me for my family to meet my phenomenal woman..." I bent my legs at my knees to be at eye level with her. "And the love of my life."

Juliette's smile melted into a dropped jaw. "The love of your life?"

I nodded, still focused on her. "Is it too soon to say that? Am I doing too much?"

Juliette shook her head and answered, "Not at all," then dropped her forehead against my chest and squealed really loudly.

"Shhh," I shushed and laughed next, wrapping my arms tighter around her. "You are so damn silly sometimes it's ridiculous."

"And I'm so wet too." She bit her bottom lip. "Ridiculously wet and for you because of what you just said."

"Oh, word?" I smirked. "Hearing stuff like that gets you wet?"

"Slip 'N Slide level of wet."

"Mmm, damn, for real?"

"Mmm-hmm." She moaned and nodded slowly. "You're gonna make me sex you in these people's bakery telling me things like that in public, Luke."

"Well, if that's the case..." I ran my thumb along the seam of her lips. "I got many more sincere facts from my heart to add to what I've told you in here today."

She kissed the pad of my thumb. "Then we need to get back to my place right now so you can whisper the rest in my ear."

"Shit." I let her go so I could snatch up her cake and the "thank you" bag it came in, while pulling her towards the bakery's exit. "We already out the door, baby."

The physical between us continues to get better as the days fall off the calendar, true. But beyond that, life with Juliette has been better than I've ever imagined.

When I met Juliette in the parking lot of her school, I met the love of my life and didn't even know it.

And though it may seem too soon to call it, when you know, you know, and I *know* Juliette is the one for me.

But we'd take things as slow as we needed to. Because I just have to see how much better things will get between us, with her and me being as open and willing to give all of ourselves to each other without limits.

My guard was finally down, and my friend Trey was right. It definitely felt more than okay for Juliette to get that side of me. She was more than deserving and I couldn't wait to see what time did with us this time around. Because the third time was indeed a charm, and Juliette was so worth the wait.

* * *

JULIETTE

I tilted my head back to measure the height of the building.

Structurally, the building was the most beautiful thing on the block and the block was quite long. Surrounded by a field of trees with bare branches that stretched toward the sky, during the warmer months, all you saw was green.

Langston University.

This was the exact view I got at twelve when my parents had to take a detour to get to one of their dry cleaners here in the city.

It was so beautiful to me.

Still was.

I shook my head and sighed, smiling, as I made my way toward the public entry lobby's turnstile doors that led into the arena.

A banner that read *"Conference Champions!"* that stretched from one end of a wall to the other guided me to the university arena.

Students posted up against the walls or walked in opposite directions, making their way through the lobby en route to connecting buildings.

LU's student body was far more diverse than at Brookville. While most of Brookville's diversity showed in our basketball team, Langston showed diversity in the various students who passed me as I walked.

I switched my slim leather briefcase onto my other hand to pull open the arena's doors and the big voices of the Ravens - Langston University's all-girl stomp and cheer squad – met me at the entrance.

I couldn't stop my smile from appearing.

Though the college basketball season ended with the NCAA National Championship Game, the girls were still in the gym. A few of them practiced routines on the hardwood floor while the others stretched on the sidelines.

I smiled with admiration as I passed them.

I wanted to be like them when I was a kid. Even at my adult age of 32, I could still appreciate how damn fly these girls really were.

I walked past the basketball hoops, headed toward the short corridor en route to Luke's office.

My editor-in-chief Mykal had given me an early print of the printed issue with Luke on the cover. His story was my best work. One of the magazine's owners, Corey Barnes, told me the exact thing. He stopped by my desk on the last day of February to gush over the story. He never spoke to me on the rare occasions he'd visit For The Culture HQ. So that was a significant sign. Corey complimenting and applauding me gave me all the confidence the editor-in-chief position would definitely be mine when Mykal steps down. Just as she planned.

I hadn't seen Luke since the previous Thursday. The new story I was working on took up a lot of my time, so I was eager to see him today.

Since the dinner at his parents' house, organized to celebrate his conference championship win, things have gotten *very* serious between us.

And to think, I was a little nervous about meeting his infamous sisters, thinking they would put me through it.

Luke and I had arrived at his parents' house, and they were the first people he introduced me to. His mother pulled me into a tight hug, and so did his father. They reminded me a lot of my parents, but a lot warmer and down to earth.

Everyone had done well with making me feel at home, but I had yet to meet his sisters.

I was bouncing my leg on the arch of my feet when Luke placed a hand on my knee to stop me.

"I know you're not nervous," he jested with a smile.

"No, of course I'm not nervous," I replied sarcastically. "Why would I be nervous to meet the sisters infamously known as your personal campus henchmen?" I turned to face him. "Is it true they used to drag girls out of your room by the hair when you lived on campus at LU?"

He hollered a laugh. "They did that like once and because that girl was stalking me and had broken into my dorm room. How'd you hear about that, anyway?"

"The crazy stories about your sisters and their ways were like tabloid news at Brookville."

All I felt was weight falling into the seat cushion beside me on the couch.

"Hey, hey, hey," came first from a woman with pecan-colored skin.

"So you're Juliette," said a taller, slimmer woman with skin the same color as Luke, next. She took a seat in the armchair across from me.

"I mean," said the third brown-skin woman who took a seat next to Luke, "She better be... sitting this close to Luke." She smiled big. "Got my

brother cheesing all wide. I can see his wisdom teeth from across the room. And just based on that, you're cool with me."

Luke snorted a laugh.

"Juliette." He pointed next to me. "This is my sister Joy." He pointed to the woman in the armchair across from me. "That's Hope." He pointed with his thumb at the woman next to him. "And this is our oldest sister, Faith."

His sisters and I all bonded with our mutual love of magazines. They were so impressed I was a journalist and contributed articles to one of their favorite publications. Even more ecstatic to learn I'd interview their brother and he would be on the cover of our latest issue.

They were far more inviting and accepting of me than I initially imagined. They made me promise to call them anytime Luke got out of line, which made me love them more. I've always wanted sisters growing up as an only child and not to jump the gun, but I was super happy with the prospect of having sisters-in-love for life.

Don't tell Luke that, though. It's driving him crazy how much his sisters and I get along. They always ask to speak to me whenever they call him and I'm around.

I arrived at the entrance of his office to find him on the couch hunched forward, forearms resting on his knees as he typed something on his phone.

Overhead behind him was a poster split into three framed collage photos, capturing the underside of a hoop with a basketball going through its net.

He wore an ash gray baseball cap to the back, a matching gray sweatsuit, and black Jordans on his feet.

"*Psst,*" I called at the door.

He raised his gaze and smiled at me, his white teeth competing with the shine in his beard.

"Guess what I have for you?"

"Something other than you?" He dropped his phone on the couch and stood to his feet and my eyes rose with him. "Because I don't care about anything else now that you're here."

"I don't know how true that is, Luke. Because what I got is a little more interesting than me." I winked, approaching his desk to set my briefcase on the surface. "Just a little."

"Oh, I doubt even a little." Luke walked up to me from behind and wrapped his arms around me, lowering his lips to my neck.

I tried to bump him away with my ass as I unzipped my briefcase. "Luke, chill."

"Uh-uh," he refused. He tried to move the top of my hooded down coat out of the way to get more access to my neck. "I haven't seen you since last Thursday because that damn story you're working on got you sitting up in that office typing shit up instead of with me sitting on my face—"

"Shhh," I shushed then giggled.

His hand crept to the crotch of my high waist stonewashed jeans.

"I miss you too." I pressed my head back against his body behind me. "But check this out!"

I held up the latest issue of For The Culture in front of us, an issue scheduled to hit newsstands the following week.

He whistled when he saw the cover, gently taking the magazine out of my hand, stepping back a bit to peruse and leaf through a few pages.

I turned to press my backside on the edge of his desk to watch him examining the cover photo of himself photographed with a cigar in his hand.

"Dope, huh?"

He peeked over at me, nodding his head, speechless.

"I told you it would be iconic."

"You did," he recalled low. "But, Juliette, baby, *damn*. I-I love it."

"I love it too."

His eyes rolled up to focus on me again.

Luke licked his lips as he took slow strides toward me, elevating my body temperature with each inch of space he eliminated between us.

He placed the magazine down on his desk beside my hip, laid a hand on my lower back, and pressed his mouth to mine.

Luke said, "And I love you," on my lips before spreading them apart with his to guide his tongue into my mouth.

And I let him.

Because I missed this man. It had only been five days apart, only eight weeks together, but I've been wanting him for over a decade.

We were making up for lost time and I was loving every moment of us playing catch-up.

He lifted me high enough to sit on his desk so he could walk between my legs. And I noticed he was stiff for me, his hard-on straining against the cotton blend fabric of his joggers.

"*Mmm*, Luke," I moaned on his lips. "I love you, too."

"*Damnnn*, Coach," we heard at the door.

We broke our kiss, and I slapped my hand to my mouth, dropping my forehead against his chest to hide as Luke laughed to himself.

"With the door open, too?! *Sheesh*," the tall young man expressed as he continued walking past the open door. "I ain't mad at it."

"Get on, Davis," Luke told him through his laugh.

Luke lowered his gaze to me and asked, "You ready to get out of here?"

I caressed his chest through his sweatshirt. "You already know I am."

I know this was still too early, but I don't know. Something told me this thing between Luke and me might last for a while. Forever, maybe? It was too soon to tell, though. But what I knew is he made time stop for me and helped me enjoy it a lot more these days. And I loved that a lot.

He was so available to me and honest with his feelings always, even when I didn't want him to be.

This thing between us was feeling like a lifetime kind of thing and I was so happy not impeding it.

He shrugged his wool coat on over his sweatsuit and draped an arm over my shoulder as we walked out of his office.

"So, what do you want for lunch?" I asked as we crossed the gym and neared the exit.

He lowered his gaze at me and licked his lips. "I was thinking... you."

I smiled big then giggled, walking through the door he held opened for me.

"What do you say to that?"

I bit back a shy smile. "I thought we were going to eat this afternoon."

"Oh." He pressed his hand to his chest. "*I'm* definitely gonna eat. I'm eating you out for sure."

I laughed, shoving him away playfully.

"Luke—"

"Juliette." He walked in front of me, blocking my path to wrap his arms around my waist and pull me close to him. "Just go 'head and say my favorite word because I promise this is a fight you are about to lose."

I arched a brow, challenging him.

"Oh, I see what this is. You want for me to beg for it? Aight, fine." He drew me closer to him. "Please, baby, *please*, may I make *you* my lunch?"

I snorted.

There in the public entry lobby of Langston U's arena, with my very own Prince Charming holding me close, begging me to have *me* for lunch.

I always wanted to go to LU and to fall in love and it finally happened, even if it wasn't exactly in the way or at the time I originally imagined it happening.

Life was clever like that, I guess.

I looked up at Luke, biting my bottom lip and nodding my answer before saying, "Okay."

He dropped his head back and whispered, "Yes," excitedly.

I laughed. "Silly."

"I'm serious though." He smirked. "See, you don't understand how much I *love* when you say..." Luke cleared his throat and in a high-pitched voice said, "Okay," mimicking me.

I couldn't help but to be a blushing mess in response and he smiled big, watching my reaction.

Luke laced his fingers with mine next and lifted the back of my palm to his lips to kiss. "Let's go, lunch."

I tossed my head back and hollered a laugh as we made our way out the glass doors in a truce.

A truce I looked forward to lasting a lifetime.

THE END.

final words

Dear Reader,

Thank you so much for purchasing your copy of *When Luke Met Juli-ette*. This story was a pleasure to write from start to finish. These two characters and their story came to me at the right time and in the right way for me to experience their evolution into fresh new romantic love in a way I don't think I've ever written before. The theme of this story was false perception. Luke and Juliette, more so Luke, allowed their perception to be shaped by inaccuracies and not by what actually was. They were always meant to be from the start and what they thought they knew about each other was wrong. Because what they had was more than what met the eye.

And thankfully, they got three opportunities to figure it out!

When I set out to write this story, the prologue attracted me to it. I loved their first interaction and how problematic it was. Luke was on Juliette's campus to pull off a rival prank and he ran right into the love of his life, literally. That's a meet cute someone tells their grandchildren about and those grandchildren build love aspirations of finding love the same way.

But not even running right into love could shatter the tough armor Luke built to maintain control of his future. And since he had the help of the people around him to keep that armor in place, it remained unmoved under all conditions, even when it was challenged in Kaysville by someone Luke considered a stranger.

Luke's shift in thinking at the end of *When Luke Met Juliette* was a necessary one. Juliette was opened to falling in love before Kaysville. After that night with Luke, she became a little hardened to protect herself from getting hurt again. I find women are encouraged and expected to seek romantic love but not really men. And this was the story for Luke. Most of his dating life, the people around him warned him to be on guard with the opposite sex because many girls his age were nothing but trouble. But he was never told about the exceptions or encouraged to seek them out.

Over a decade later, Luke realizes his life of success doesn't satisfy his need for companionship.

So, he was already halfway there to opening his heart just in time for his reunion with Juliette, being the last of his friends to find romantic love. His sincere friendship with Trey played a significant role in Luke calling Juliette after she stormed out of Mon Ami. Instead of showing up with their hearts opened, the both of them arrived at the restaurant on guard, neither one of them wanting to back down. I think it showed growth when he called her and acknowledged his role in her walking out of their interview. Because had it been the old Luke, there wasn't any telling if the two would ever see each other again. But his desire in wanting to see how real things could be with Juliette after life brought them together for the third time, in another unlikely way, was the actual driving force.

Loved how open he was at the end, loved even more that he allowed Juliette into his heart in a way she's truly desired.

Their happily ever after was a little new for me because their relationship was very new. While most of my epilogues take us a few months into the future, often a year, we're catching up with Luke and Juliette weeks later in their epilogue. They aren't exes, and they aren't even old schoolmates. The only time they saw one another was at least once a year (twice when Juliette got the chance to cheer at Langston for BU's away games), when their schools played against each other. In essence, Luke and Juliette were strangers who have felt this pull – this energy *wink, wink* – to each other for many years that made them feel like *literally feel* as if they've known each other forever. Their relationship is so new, but they can sense at this point that their union isn't anything flimsy. And it isn't. It's energy! Being that their relationship is new, though, there's so many future opportunities to catch up with these two, in my mind at least. So I look forward to doing that.

In the middle of creating *When Luke Met Juliette,* they inspired me to work on another story with a related character from WLMJ (who I'll reveal much later). So, I created The Energy series and to make WLMJ a part of that series. Though there are no other stories for Luke and Juliette currently, you can expect to see updates from them since Juliette will assume the role of editor-in-chief at For The Culture Magazine, a magazine I feature often in my stories, and Luke is a coach at a fictional university I create stories around often as well.

Like I said, *When Luke Met Juliette* was a pleasure to write and there's so much more I can say about this story, but I'd much rather leave your interpretations of this tale up to you.

How did you feel about this story? The best way to express that is in a review! If you care to, please consider leaving a review of *When Luke Met Juliette* on either Amazon or Goodreads or both! I'd appreciate it.

Thank you so much for reading.

If this is your first book by me, I'd like to think you're a Brookelynite now. So, welcome!

To my readers who have been reading from a book or several books ago, I thank you so much for your continued support. As I've been saying, we are at book #35, a milestone, and how far we have come.

New and returning readers, thank you for joining me on this journey. And as always, I'll see you at the end of the next book!

Love,
Brookelyn.

book club questions

1. What was your first impression of Luke Lockett?

2. What was your first impression of Juliette Hart?

3. After reading the prologue, did you expect for the two to be enemies?

4. Do you think the situation would have been different if Luke knew Juliette didn't really love Brookville University the way he assumed?

5. What was your favorite moment from *When Luke Met Juliette*?

6. What was your favorite takeaway after reading this story?

7. What did you think of Luke's three older sisters? Do you think they played a positive or negative role in his life?

8. Do you think it was right for the people in Luke's life to encourage him to keep his guard up around the opposite sex?

9. Do you think their relationship is something that will last a lifetime?

10. Do you think it should've taken so long for Luke and Juliette to see what they finally saw in each other?

character cameos

In the order they appeared or were mentioned in When Luke Met Juliette...

Mykal Jones

Envy

So This is Love

Desmond Ellis III

Envy

Coach Walters

So This is Love

Brookelyn wrote her first short story when she was a sophomore in high school. Back then she discovered how using her experience as a teen living in Brooklyn to create romantic shorts was just as exciting to her as retail shopping and going on dates. After starting her first semester of college two years later, Brookelyn's creative writing became more of a hobby and something to escape the stress of midterms and finals.

Now in her 30s as a freelance writer, penning short stories and novellas is her everything. While her experience with writing has evolved for the better, her undying love for creating fiction remains unchanged. Brookelyn's focus is on creating contemporary women's fiction with characters based in urban settings. Her stories chronicle the emotional journeys and erotic experiences of women today through her characters and the scenarios they're thrown into.

The motivation behind her brand of writing has a lot to do with what she discovered storytelling provided for her - an escape. Her goal with her work is to create characters and urban worlds that offer a great escape for fiction readers looking for a break from the daily grind of adulting and who prefer to relax with good books and short stories. When she's not freelance copywriting, doing yoga, or showing her husband, son, and daughter lots of love, she can be found sitting at her computer desk, with her legs folded, and a cup of coffee (or a glass of wine) at arm's reach as she types or edits her latest short or novella.